A WORI
TOO DA
PꞭꞮꝓꝒꝭ?

Here is a tale of the frightening future. Science has eliminated all possibility of war. People everywhere have enough food to eat. Could mankind have truly found paradise at last? Not likely. Because of these "boons to mankind," the Earth has become hopelessly over-populated and its resources are now being pushed to the limit. The government, though, has devised a last-ditch scheme to solve the problem. A scheme that has more than its fair share of dissenters.

This Crowded Earth is an intrigue-filled tale of the far-off future, as told by one of the science fiction and fantasy's most brilliant writers, Robert Bloch.

FOR A COMPLETE SECOND NOVEL, TURN TO PAGE 85

ABOUT ROBERT BLOCH

Robert Bloch…

…got his start by writing a fan letter to horror fiction legend H. P. Lovecraft when he was only sixteen years old. Lovecraft wrote back and emboldened the youthful Bloch, who soon started writing tales of supernatural fiction. Submissions to *Weird Tales* followed shortly thereafter, kicking off one of the most brilliant writing careers in the history of the horror, science fiction, and mystery genres. Bloch is best known for his terror tales, his masterpiece of course being the much-heralded, *Psycho*. But he was also known for occasionally turning out some dandy science fiction yarns and wrote many fine stories for pulp and digest magazines like *Amazing Stories* and *Imagination*. He was once quoted as saying, "Despite my ghoulish reputation, I really have the heart of a small boy. I keep it in a jar on my desk." Robert Bloch passed away in 1994 at the age of 77.

THIS CROWDED EARTH

By
ROBERT BLOCH

ARMCHAIR FICTION
PO Box 4369, Medford, Oregon 97501-0168

*For more information about Armchair Books and products, visit our
website at…*

www.armchairfiction.com

Or email us at…

armchairfiction@yahoo.com

CHAPTER ONE
Harry Collins—1997

The telescreen lit up promptly at eight a.m. Smiling Brad came on with his usual greeting. "Good morning—it's a beautiful day in Chicagee!"

Harry Collins rolled over and twitched off the receiver. "This I doubt," he muttered. He sat up and reached into the closet for his clothing.

Visitors—particularly feminine ones—were always exclaiming over the advantages of Harry's apartment. "So convenient," they would say. "Everything handy, right within reach. And think of all the extra steps you save!"

Of course most of them were just being polite and trying to cheer Harry up. They knew damned well that he wasn't living in one room through any choice of his own. The Housing Act was something you just couldn't get around; not in Chicagee these days. A bachelor was entitled to one room—no more and no less. And even though Harry was making a speedy buck at the agency, he couldn't hope to beat the regulations.

There was only one way to beat them and that was to get married. Marriage would automatically entitle him to two rooms—*if* he could find them someplace.

More than a few of his feminine visitors had hinted at just that, but Harry didn't respond. Marriage was no solution, the way he figured it. He knew that he couldn't hope to locate a two-room apartment any closer than eighty miles away. It was bad enough driving forty miles to and from work every morning and night without doubling the distance. If he did find a bigger place, that would mean a three-hour trip each way on one of the commutrains, and the commutrains were murder. The Black Hole of Calcutta, on wheels.

5

But then, everything was murder, Harry reflected, as he stepped from the toilet to the sink, from the sink to the stove, from the stove to the table.

Powdered eggs for breakfast. That was murder, too. But it was a fast, cheap meal, easy to prepare, and the ingredients didn't waste a lot of storage space. The only trouble was, he hated the way they tasted. Harry wished he had time to eat his breakfasts in a restaurant. He could afford the price, but he couldn't afford to wait in line more than a half-hour or so. His office schedule at the agency started promptly at ten-thirty. And he didn't get out until three-thirty; it was a long, hard five-hour day. Sometimes he wished he worked in the New Philly area, where a four-hour day was the rule. But he supposed that wouldn't mean any real saving in time, because he'd have to live further out. What was the population in New Philly now? Something like 63,000,000, wasn't it? Chicagee was much smaller—only 38,000,000, this year.

This year. Harry shook his head and took a gulp of the Instantea. Yes, this year the population was 38,000,000, and the boundaries of the community extended north to what used to be the old Milwaukee and south past Gary. What would it be like *next* year, and the year following?

Lately that question had begun to haunt Harry. He couldn't quite figure out why. After all, it was none of his business, really. He had a good job, security, a nice place just two hours from the Loop. He even drove his own car. What more could he ask?

And why did he have to start the day like this, with a blinding headache?

Harry finished his Instantea and considered the matter. Yes, it was beginning again, just as it had on almost every morning for the past month. He'd sit down at the table, eat his usual breakfast, and end up with a headache. Why?

It wasn't the food; for a while he'd deliberately varied his diet, but that didn't make any difference. And he'd had his usual monthly checkup not more than ten days ago, only to be assured there was nothing wrong with him. Still, the headaches persisted. Every morning, when he'd sit down and jerk his head to the left like this—

That was it. Jerking his head to the left. It always seemed to trigger the pain. But why? And where had he picked up this habit of jerking his head to the left?

Harry didn't know.

He glanced at his watch. It was almost nine, now. High time that he got started. He reached over to the interapartment video and dialled the garage downstairs.

"Bill," he said. "Can you bring my car around to Number Three?"

The tiny face in the hand-screen grinned sheepishly. "Mr. Collins, ain't it? Gee, I'm sorry, Mr. Collins. Night crew took on a new man, he must have futzed around with the lists, and I can't find your number."

Harry sighed. "It's one-eight-seven-three-dash-five," he said. "Light blue Pax, two-seater. Do you want the license number, too?"

"No, just your parking number. I'll recognize it when I see it. But God only knows what level it's on. That night man really—"

"Never mind," Harry interrupted. "How soon?"

"Twenty minutes or so. Maybe half an hour."

"Half an hour? I'll be late. Hurry it up!"

Harry clicked the video and shook his head. Half an hour! Well, you had to expect these things if you wanted to be independent and do your own driving today. If he wanted to work his priority through the office, he could get his application honored on the I.C. Line within a month. But the I.C. was just another commutrain, and he couldn't take it.

Standing and swaying for almost two hours, fighting the crowds, battling his way in and out of the sidewalk escalators. Besides, there was always the danger of being crushed. He'd seen an old man trampled to death on a Michigan Boulevard escalator-feeder, and he'd never forgotten it.

Being afraid was only a partial reason for his reluctance to change. The worst thing, for Harry, was the thought of all those people; the forced bodily contact, the awareness of smothered breathing, odors, and the crushing confinement of flesh against flesh. It was bad enough in the lines, or on the streets. The commutrain was just too much.

Yet, as a small boy, Harry could remember the day when he'd loved such trips. Sitting there looking out of the window as the scenery whirled past—that was always a thrill when you were a little kid. How long ago had that been? More than twenty years, wasn't it?

Now there weren't any seats, and no windows. Which was just as well, probably, because the scenery didn't whirl past any more, either. Instead, there was a stop at every station on the line, and a constant battle as people jockeyed for position to reach the exit-doors in time.

No, the car was better.

Harry reached for a container in the cabinet and poured out a couple of aspirystamines. That ought to help the headache. At least until he got to the office. Then he could start with the daily quota of yellowjackets. Meanwhile, getting out on the street might help him, too. A shame there wasn't a window in this apartment, but then, what good would it do, really? All he could see through it would be the next apartment.

He shrugged and picked up his coat. Nine-thirty, time to go downstairs. Maybe the car would be located sooner than Bill had promised; after all, he had nine assistants, and not everybody went to work on this first daylight shift.

Harry walked down the hall and punched the elevator button. He looked at the indicator, watched the red band move towards the numeral of this floor, then sweep past it.

"Full up!" he muttered. "Oh, well."

He reached out and touched both sides of the corridor. That was another thing he disliked; these narrow corridors. Two people could scarcely squeeze past one another without touching. Of course, it did save space to build apartments this way, and space was at a premium. But Harry couldn't get used to it. Now he remembered some of the old buildings that were still around when he was a little boy—

The headache seemed to be getting worse instead of better. Harry looked at the indicator above the other elevator entrance. The red band was crawling upward, passing him to stop on 48. That was the top floor. Now it was moving down, down; stopping on 47, 46, 45, 44, 43, and—here it was!

"Stand back, please!" said the tape. Harry did his best to oblige, but there wasn't much room. A good two dozen of his upstairs neighbors jammed the compartment. Harry thought he recognized one or two of the men, but he couldn't be sure. There were so many people, so many faces. After a while it got so they all seemed to look alike. Yes, and breathed alike, and felt alike when you were squeezed up against them, and you were always being squeezed up against them, wherever you went. And you could smell them, and hear them wheeze and cough, and you went falling down with them into a bottomless pit where your head began to throb and throb and it was hard to move away from all that heat and pressure. It was hard enough just to keep from screaming—

Then the door opened and Harry was catapulted out into the lobby. The mob behind him pushed and clawed because they were in a hurry; they were always in a hurry these days, and if you got in their way they'd trample you down like that old man had been trampled down; there was no room for one man in a crowd any more.

Harry blinked and shook his head.

He gripped the edge of the wall and clung there in an effort to avoid being swept out of the lobby completely. His hands were sticky with perspiration. They slipped off as he slowly inched his way back through the crush of the mob.

"Wait for me!" he called. "Wait for me, I'm going down!" But his voice was lost in the maelstrom of sound just as his body was lost in the maelstrom of motion. Besides, an automatic elevator cannot hear. It is merely a mechanism that goes up and down, just like the other mechanisms that go in and out, or around and around, and you get caught up in them the way a squirrel gets caught in a squirrel-cage and you race and race, and the best you can hope for is to keep up with the machinery.

The elevator door clanged shut before Harry could reach it. He waited for another car to arrive, and this time he stood aside as the crowd emerged, then darted in behind them.

The car descended to the first garage level, and Harry stood gulping gratefully in the comparative isolation. There weren't more than ten people accompanying him.

He emerged on the ramp, gave his number to the attendant, and waved at Bill in his office. Bill seemed to recognize him; at least he nodded, briefly. No sense trying to talk—not in this sullen subterranea, filled with the booming echo of exhausts, the despairing shriek of brakes. Headlights flickered in the darkness as cars whirled past, ascending and descending on the loading platforms. The signal systems winked from the walls, and tires screeched defiance to the warning bells.

Old-fashioned theologians, Harry remembered, used to argue whether there really was a Hell, and if so, had it been created by God or the Devil? Too bad they weren't around today to get an answer to their questions. There *was* a Hell, and it had been created by General Motors.

Harry's temples began to throb. Through blurred eyes, he saw the attendant beckoning him down the line to a platform marked *Check-Out #3*. He stood there with a cluster of others, waiting.

What was the matter with him today, anyway? First the headache, and now his feet were hurting. Standing around waiting, that's what did it. This eternal waiting. When he was a kid, the grownups were always complaining about the long seven-hour work days and how they cut into their leisure time. Well, maybe they had reason to gripe, but at least there *was* some leisure before work began or after it was through. Now that extra time was consumed in waiting. Standing in line, standing in crowds, wearing yourself out doing nothing.

Still, this time it wasn't really so bad. Within ten minutes the light blue Pax rolled up before him. Harry climbed in as the attendant slid out from behind the wheel and prepared to leave.

Then a fat man appeared, running along the ramp. He gestured wildly with a plump thumb. Harry nodded briefly, and the fat man hurled himself into the seat beside him and slammed the door.

They were off. Harry read the signals impatiently, waiting for the green *Go*. The moment he saw it he gunned his motor and got the car up to twenty-two and zipped away.

That's what he liked, that's what he always waited for. Of course it was dangerous, here in the tunnel system under the garage, but Harry always got a thrill out of speed. The Pax could do thirty-five or even forty, probably, on a theoretical open road. Still, twenty-two was enough to satisfy Harry.

He whizzed up the ramp, turned, headed for the street-level, then braked and waited for the signal to emerge.

Harsh sunlight pierced the smog and he felt his eyes watering. Now the street noises assailed his ears; the grinding of gears, the revving of motors. But at least the total volume was lower, and with the windows tightly closed against the acrid air, he could hear.

Turning to the fat man beside him he said, "Hello, Frazer. What's the urgency?"

"Got to get downtown before eleven," the fat man answered. "Board meeting today, but I forgot about it. Knew I wouldn't have time to wait for the car, and I was hoping I'd find someone who'd give me a lift. Lucky for me that you came along when you did."

Harry nodded but did not reply. At the moment he was trying to edge into the traffic beyond. It flowed, bumper to bumper, in a steady stream; a stream moving at the uniform and prescribed rate of fifteen miles per hour. He released his brakes and the Pax nosed forward until a truck sounded its horn in ominous warning. The noise hurt Harry's head; he winced and grimaced.

"What's the matter?" asked Frazer.

"Headache," Harry muttered. He menaced a Chevsoto with his bumper. "Damn it, I thought they didn't allow those big four-passenger jobs on this arterial during rush hours!" Gradually he managed to turn until he was in the righthand lane. "There," he said. "We're off."

And so they were, for all of three minutes, with the speed set at fifteen on autopilot. Then a signal went into action somewhere up ahead, and the procession halted. Harry flicked his switch. As was customary, horns sounded indignantly on all sides—a mechanical protest against a mechanical obstruction. Harry winced again.

"Hangover?" Frazer asked, solicitously. "Try aspirystamine."

Harry shook his head. "No hangover. And I've already taken three, thanks. Nothing does any good. So I guess it's just up to you."

"Up to me?" Frazer was genuinely puzzled. "What can I do about your headaches?"

"You're on the Board of City Planners, aren't you?"

"That's right."

"Well, I've got a suggestion for you to give to them. Tell them to start planning to drop a couple of heavy thermo-nucs on this area. Clean out twenty or thirty million people. We'd never miss 'em."

Frazer chuckled wryly. "I wish I had a buck for every time I've heard *that* suggestion."

"Ever stop to think why you hear it so often? It's because everybody feels the same way—we can't take being hemmed in like this."

"Well, a bomb wouldn't help. You know that." Frazer pursed his lips. "Robertson figured out what would happen, with the chain-reaction."

Harry glanced sideways at his companion as the car started forward once again. "I've always wondered about that," he said. "Seriously, I mean. Is the story really true, or is it just some more of this government propaganda you fellows like to hand out?"

Frazer sighed. "It's true, all right. There was a scientist named Robertson, and he did come up with the thermo-nuc formula, way back in '75. Proved it, too. Use what he developed and the chain-reaction would never end. Scientists in other countries tested the theory and agreed; there was no collusion, it just worked out that way on a practical basis. Hasn't been a war since—what more proof do you want?"

"Well, couldn't they just use some of the old-fashioned hydrogen bombs?"

"Be sensible, man! Once a war started, no nation could resist the temptation to go all-out. Fortunately, everyone realizes that. So we have peace. Permanent peace."

"I'll take a good war anytime, in preference to this."

"Harry, you don't know what you're talking about. You aren't so young that you can't remember what it was like in the old days. Everybody living in fear, waiting for the bombs to fall. People dying of disease and worried about dying from radiation and fallout. All the international rivalries, the power-politics, the eternal pressures and constant crises. Nobody in his right mind would want to go back to *that*. We've come a mighty long way in the last twenty years or so."

Harry switched to autopilot and sat back. "Maybe that's the trouble," he said. "Maybe we've come too far, too fast. I wasn't kidding about dropping those thermo-nucs, either. *Something* has to be done. We can't go on like this indefinitely. Why doesn't the Board come up with an answer?"

Frazer shrugged his heavy shoulders. "You think we haven't tried, aren't trying now? We're aware of the situation as well as you are—and then some. But there's no easy solution. The population just keeps growing, that's all. No war to cut it down, contagious diseases at a minimum, average life-expectancy up to ninety years or better. Naturally, this results in a problem. But a bomb won't help bring about any permanent solution. Besides, this isn't a local matter, or even a national one. It's global. What do you think those summit meetings are all about?"

"What about birth control?" Harry asked. "Why don't they really get behind an emigration movement?"

"We can't limit procreation by law. You know that." Frazer peered out at the swarming streams on the sidewalk levels. "It's more than a religious or a political question—it's a social one. People want kids. They can afford them. Besides, the Housing Act is set up so that having kids is just about the only way you can ever get into larger living-quarters."

"Couldn't they try reverse-psychology? I mean, grant priority to people who are willing to be sterilized?"

"They tried it, on a limited experimental scale, about three years ago out on the West Coast."

"I never heard anything about it."

"Damned right you didn't," Frazer replied, grimly. "They kept the whole project under wraps, and for a good reason. The publicity might have wrecked the Administration."

"What happened?"

"What do you suppose happened? There were riots. Do you think a man and his wife and three kids, living in three rooms, liked the idea of standing by and watching a sterilized couple enjoy a four-room place with lawn space? Things got pretty ugly, let me tell you. There was a rumor going around that the country was in the hands of homosexuals—the churches were up in arms—and if that wasn't bad enough, we had to face up to the primary problem. There just wasn't, just isn't, enough *space*. Not in areas suitable for maintaining a population. Mountains are still mountains and deserts are still deserts. Maybe we can put up housing in such regions, but who can live there? Even with decentralization going full blast, people must live within reasonable access to their work. No, we're just running out of room."

Again the car halted on signal. Over the blasting of the horns, Harry repeated his query about emigration.

Frazer shook his head, but made no attempt to reply until the horns had quieted and they were under way once more.

"As for emigration, we're just getting some of our own medicine in return. About eighty years ago, we clamped down and closed the door on immigrants; established a quota. Now the same quota is being used against us, and you can't really blame other nations for it. They're facing worse population increases than we are. Look at the African Federation, and what's happened there, in spite of all the wealth! And South America is even worse, in spite of all the reclamation projects. Fifteen years ago, when they cleared out the Amazon Basin, they thought they'd have enough room for fifty years to come. And now look at it--two hundred million, that's the latest figure we've got."

"So what's the answer?" Harry asked.

"I don't know. If it wasn't for hydroponics and the Ag Culture controls, we'd be licked right now. As it is, we can still supply enough food, and the old supply-and-demand takes care of the economy as a whole. I have no recommendations for an overall solution, or even a regional one. My job, the Board's job, is regulating housing and traffic and transportation in Chicagee. That's about all you can expect us to handle."

Again they jolted to a stop and the horns howled all around them. Harry sat there until a muscle in the side of his jaw began to twitch. Suddenly he pounded on the horn with both fists.

"Shut up!" he yelled. "For the love of Heaven, shut up!"

Abruptly he slumped back. "Sorry," he mumbled. "It's my damned headache. I—I've got to get out of this."

"Job getting you down?"

"No. It's a good job. At least everybody tells me so. Twenty-five hours a week, three hundred bucks. The car. The room. The telescreen and liquor and yellowjackets. Plenty of time to kill. Unless it's the time that's killing me."

"But—what do you *want*?"

Harry stepped on the accelerator and they inched along. Now the street widened into eight traffic lanes and the big semis joined the procession on the edge of the downtown area.

"I want out," Harry said. "Out of this."

"Don't you ever visit the National Preserves?" Frazer asked.

"Sure I do. Fly up every vacation. Take a tame plane to a tame government resort and catch my quota of two tame fish. Great sport! If I got married, I'd be entitled to four tame fish. But that's not what I want. I want what my father used to talk about. I want to drive into the country, without a permit, mind you; just to drive wherever I like. I want to see cows and chickens and trees and lakes and sky."

"You sound like a Naturalist."

"Don't sneer. Maybe the Naturalists are right. Maybe we ought to cut out all this phoney progress and phoney peace that passeth all understanding. I'm no liberal, don't get me wrong, but sometimes I think the Naturalists have the only answer."

"But what can you do about it?" Frazer murmured. "Suppose for the sake of argument that they *are* right. How can you change things? We can't just *will* ourselves to stop growing, and we can't legislate against biology. More people, in better health, with more free time, are just bound to have more offspring. It's inevitable, under the circumstances. And neither you nor I nor anyone has the right to condemn millions upon millions of others to death through war or disease."

"I know," Harry said. "It's hopeless, I guess. All the same, I want out." He wet his lips. "Frazer, you're on the Board here. You've got connections higher up. If I could only get a chance to transfer to Ag Culture, go on one of those farms as a worker—"

Frazer shook his head. "Sorry, Harry. You know the situation there, I'm sure. Right now there's roughly ninety million approved applications on file. Everybody wants to get into Ag Culture."

"But couldn't I just buy some land, get a government contract for foodstuffs?"

"Have you got the bucks? A minimum forty acres leased from one of the farm corporations will cost you two hundred thousand at the very least, not counting equipment." He paused. "Besides, there's Vocational Apt. What did your tests show?"

"You're right," Harry said. "I'm supposed to be an agency man. An agency man until I die. Or retire on my pension, at fifty, and sit in my little room for the next fifty years, turning on the telescreen every morning to hear some loudmouthed liar tell me it's a beautiful day in Chicagee. Who knows, maybe by that time we'll have a hundred billion people enjoying peace and progress and prosperity. All sitting in little rooms and—"

"Watch out!" Frazer grabbed the wheel. "You nearly hit that truck." He waited until Harry's face relaxed before relinquishing his grip. "Harry, you'd better go in for a checkup. It isn't just a headache with you, is it?"

"You're not fooling," Harry told him. "It isn't just a headache."

He began to think about what it *really* was, and that helped a little. It helped him get through the worst part, which was the downtown traffic and letting Frazer off and listening to Frazer urge him to see a doctor.

Then he got to the building parking area and let them take his car away and bury it down in the droning darkness where the horns hooted and the headlights glared.

Harry climbed the ramp and mingled with the ten-thirty shift on its way up to the elevators. Eighteen elevators in his building, to serve eighty floors. Nine of the elevators were express to the fiftieth floor, three were express to sixty-five. He wanted one of the latter, and so did the mob. The crushing, clinging mob. They pressed and panted the way

18

mobs always do; mobs that lynch and torture and dance around bonfires and guillotines and try to drag you down to trample you to death because they can't stand you if your name is Harry and you want to be different.

They hate you because you don't like powdered eggs and the telescreen and a beautiful day in Chicagee. And they stare at you because your forehead hurts and the muscle in your jaw twitches and they know you want to scream as you go up, up, up, and try to think why you get a headache from jerking your head to the left.

Then Harry was at the office door and they said good morning when he came in, all eighty of the typists in the outer office working their electronic machines and offering him their electronic smiles, including the girl he had made electronic love to last Saturday night and who wanted him to move into a two-room marriage and have children, lots of children who could enjoy peace and progress and prosperity.

Harry snapped out of it, going down the corridor. Only a few steps more and he'd be safe in his office, his own private office, almost as big as his apartment. And there would be liquor, and the yellowjackets in the drawer. That would help. Then he could get to work.

What was today's assignment? He tried to remember. It was Wilmer-Klibby, wasn't it? Telescreenads for Wilmer-Klibby, makers of window-glass.

Window-glass.

He opened his office door and then slammed it shut behind him. For a minute everything blurred, and then he could remember.

Now he knew what caused him to jerk his head, what gave him the headaches when he did so. Of course. That was it.

When he sat down at the table for breakfast in the morning he turned his head to the left because he'd always done so, ever since he was a little boy. A little boy, in what was then Wheaton, sitting at the breakfast table and looking out of the window. Looking out at summer sunshine, spring rain, autumn haze, the white wonder of newfallen snow.

He'd never broken himself of the habit. He still looked to the left every morning, just as he had today. But there was no window any more. There was only a blank wall. And beyond it, the smog and the clamor and the crowds.

Window-glass. Wilmer-Klibby had problems. Nobody was buying window-glass any more. Nobody except the people who put up buildings like this. There were still windows on the top floors, just like the window here in his office.

Harry stepped over to it, moving very slowly because of his head. It hurt to keep his eyes open, but he wanted to stare out of the window. Up this high you could see above the smog. You could see the sun like a radiant jewel packed in the cotton cumulus of clouds. If you opened the window you could feel fresh air against your forehead, you could breathe it in and breathe out the headache.

But you didn't dare look down. Oh, no, never look *down*, because then you'd see the buildings all around you. The buildings below, black and sooty, their jagged outlines like the stumps of rotten teeth. And they stretched off in all directions, as far as the eye could attain; row after row of rotten teeth grinning up from the smog-choked throat of the streets. From the maw of the city far below came this faint but endless howling, this screaming of traffic and toil. And you couldn't help it, you breathed *that* in too, along with the fresh air, and it poisoned you and it did more than make your head ache. It made your heart ache and it made your soul sick, and it made you close your eyes and your lungs and your brain against it.

Harry reeled, but he knew this was the only way. *Close your brain against it.* And then, when you opened your eyes again, maybe you could see the way things used to be—

It was snowing out and it was a *wet* snow, the very best kind for snowballs and making a snowman, and the whole gang would come out after school.

But there was no school, this was Saturday, and the leaves were russet and gold and red so that it looked as if all the trees in the world were on fire. And you could scuff when you walked and pile up fallen leaves from the grass and roll in them.

And it was swell to roll down the front lawn in summer, just roll right down to the edge of the sidewalk like it was a big hill and let Daddy catch you at the bottom, laughing.

Mamma laughed too, and she said, *Look, it's springtime, the lilacs are out, do you want to touch the pretty lilacs, Harry?*

And Harry didn't quite understand what she was saying, but he reached out and they were purple and smelled of rain and soft sweetness and they were just beyond the window, if he reached a little further he could touch them—

And then the snow and the leaves and the grass and the lilacs disappeared, and Harry could see the rotten teeth again, leering and looming and snapping at him. They were going to bite, they were going to chew, they were going to devour, and he couldn't stop them, couldn't stop himself. He was falling into the howling jaws of the city.

His last conscious effort was a desperate attempt to gulp fresh air into his lungs before he pinwheeled down. Fresh air was good for headaches...

CHAPTER TWO
Harry Collins—1998

It took them ten seconds to save Harry from falling, but it took him over ten weeks to regain his balance.

In fact, well over two months had passed before he could fully realize just what had happened, or where he was now.

They must have noticed something was wrong with him that morning at the office, because two supervisors and an exec rushed in and caught him just as he was going out of the window. And then they had sent him away, sent him *here*.

"This is fine," he told Dr. Manschoff. "If I'd known how well they treated you, I'd have gone couch-happy years ago."

Dr. Manschoff's plump face was impassive, but the little laugh-lines deepened around the edges of his eyes. "Maybe that's why we take such care not to publicize our recent advances in mental therapy," he said. "Everybody would want to get into a treatment center, and then where would we be?"

Harry nodded, staring past the doctor's shoulder, staring out of the wide window at the broad expanse of rolling countryside beyond.

"I still don't understand, though," he murmured. "How can you possibly manage to maintain an institution like this, with all the space and the luxuries? The inmates seem to lead a better life than the adjusted individuals outside. It's topsy-turvy."

"Perhaps." Dr. Manschoff's fingers formed a pudgy steeple. "But then, so many things seem to be topsy-turvy nowadays, don't they? Wasn't it the realization of this fact which precipitated your own recent difficulties?"

"Almost precipitated me bodily out of that window," Harry admitted, cheerfully. "And that's another thing. I was sent here, I suppose, because I'd attempted suicide, gone into shock, temporary amnesia, something like that."

"Something like that," the doctor echoed, contemplating his steeple.

"But you didn't give me any treatment," Harry continued. "Oh, I was kept under sedation for a while, I realize that. And you and some of the other staff-members talked to me.

But mainly I just rested in a nice big room and ate nice big meals."

"So?" The steeple's fleshy spire collapsed.

"So what I want to know is, when does the real treatment start? When do I go into analysis, or chemotherapy, and all that?"

Dr. Manschoff shrugged. "Do you think you need those things now?"

Harry gazed out at the sunlight beyond the window, half-squinting and half-frowning. "No, come to think of it, I don't believe I do. I feel better now than I have in years."

His companion leaned back. "Meaning that for years you felt all wrong. Because you were constricted, physically, psychically, and emotionally. You were cramped, squeezed in a vise until the pressure became intolerable. But now that pressure has been removed. As a result you no longer suffer, and there is no need to seek escape in death or denial of identity.

"This radical change of attitude has been brought about here in just a little more than two months' time. And yet you're asking me when the 'real treatment' begins."

"I guess I've already had the real treatment then, haven't I?"

"That is correct. Prolonged analysis or drastic therapy is unnecessary. We've merely given you what you seemed to need."

"I'm very grateful," Harry said. "But how can you afford to do it?"

Dr. Manschoff built another temple to an unknown god. He inspected the architecture critically now as he spoke. "Because your problem is a rarity," he said.

"Rarity? I'd have thought millions of people would be breaking down every month. The Naturalists say—"

The doctor nodded wearily. "I know what they say. But let's dismiss rumors and consider facts. Have you ever read any *official* report stating that the number of cases of mental illness ran into the millions?"

"No, I haven't."

"For that matter, do you happen to know of *anyone* who was ever sent to a treatment center such as this?"

"Well, of course, everybody goes in to see the medics for regular check-ups and this includes an interview with a psych. But if they're in bad shape he just puts them on extra tranquilizers. I guess sometimes he reviews their Vocational Apt tests and shifts them over into different jobs in other areas."

Dr. Manschoff bowed his head in reverence above the steeple, as if satisfied with the labors he had wrought. "That is roughly correct. And I believe, if you search your memory, you won't recall even a mention of a treatment center. This sort of place is virtually extinct, nowadays. There are still some institutions for those suffering from functional mental disorders—paresis, senile dementia, congenital abnormalities. But regular check-ups and preventative therapy take care of the great majority. We've ceased concentrating on the result of mental illnesses and learned to attack the causes.

"It's the old yellow fever problem all over again, you see. Once upon a time, physicians dealt exclusively with treatment of yellow fever patients. Then they shifted their attention to the *source* of the disease. They went after the mosquitoes, drained the swamps, and the yellow fever problem vanished.

"That's been our approach in recent years. We've developed *social* therapy, and so the need for individual therapy has diminished.

"What were the sources of the tensions producing mental disturbances? Physical and financial insecurity, the threat of war, the aggressive patterns of a competitive society, the unresolved Oedipus-situation rooted in the old-style family relationship. These were the swamps where the mosquitoes buzzed and bit. Most of the swamps have been dredged, most of the insects exterminated.

"Today we're moving into a social situation where nobody goes hungry, nobody is jobless or unprovided for, nobody needs to struggle for status. Vocational Apt determines a man's rightful place and function in society, and there's no longer the artificial distinction imposed by race, color or creed. War is a thing of the past. Best of all, the old-fashioned 'home-life,' with all of its unhealthy emotional ties, is being replaced by sensible conditioning when a child reaches school age. The umbilical cord is no longer a permanent leash, a strangler's noose, or a silver-plated life-line stretching back to the womb."

Harry Collins nodded. "I suppose only the exceptional cases ever need to go to a treatment center like this."

"Exactly."

"But what makes *me* one of the exceptions? Is it because of the way the folks brought me up, in a small town, with all the old-fashioned books and everything? Is that why I hated confinement and conformity so much? Is it because of all the years I spent reading? And why—"

Dr. Manschoff stood up. "You tempt me," he said. "You tempt me strongly. As you can see, I dearly love a lecture—and a captive audience. But right now, the audience must not remain captive. I prescribe an immediate dose of freedom."

"You mean I'm to leave here?"

"Is that what you want to do?"

"Frankly, no. Not if it means going back to my job."

"That hasn't been decided upon. We can discuss the problem later, and perhaps we can go into the answers to those questions you just posed. But at the moment, I'd suggest you stay with us, though without the restraint of remaining in your room or in the wards. In other words, I want you to start going outside again."

"Outside?"

"You'll find several square miles of open country just beyond the doors here. You're at liberty to wander around and enjoy yourself. Plenty of fresh air and sunshine—come and go as you wish. I've already issued instructions which permit you to keep your own hours. Meals will be available when you desire them."

"You're very kind."

"Nonsense. I'm prescribing what you need. And when the time comes, we'll arrange to talk again. You know where to find me."

Dr. Manschoff dismantled his steeple and placed a half of the roof in each trouser-pocket.

And Harry Collins went outdoors.

It was wonderful just to be free and alone—like returning to that faraway childhood in Wheaton once again. Harry appreciated every minute of it during the first week of his wandering.

But Harry wasn't a child any more, and after a week he began to wonder instead of wander.

The grounds around the treatment center were more than spacious; they seemed absolutely endless. No matter how far he walked during the course of a day, Harry had never encountered any walls, fences or artificial barriers; there was nothing to stay his progress but the natural barriers of high, steeply-slanting precipices which seemed to rim all sides of a vast valley. Apparently the center itself was set in the middle of a large canyon—a canyon big enough to contain an airstrip for helicopter landings. The single paved road leading from the main buildings terminated at the airstrip, and Harry saw helicopters arrive and depart from time to time; apparently they brought in food and supplies.

As for the center itself, it consisted of four large structures, two of which Harry was familiar with. The largest was made up of apartments for individual patients, and staffed by nurses and attendants. Harry's own room was here, on the second floor, and from the beginning he'd been allowed to roam around the communal halls below at will.

The second building was obviously administrative—Dr. Manschoff's private office was situated therein, and presumably the other staff-members operated out of here.

The other two buildings were apparently inaccessible; not guarded or policed or even distinguished by signs prohibiting access, but merely locked and unused. At least, Harry had found the doors locked when—out of normal curiosity—he had ventured to approach them. Nor had he ever seen anyone enter or leave the premises. Perhaps these structures were unnecessary under the present circumstances, and had been built for future accommodations.

Still, Harry couldn't help wondering.

And now, on this particular afternoon, he sat on the bank of the little river which ran through the valley, feeling the mid-summer sun beating down upon his forehead and staring down at the eddying current with its ripples and reflections.

Ripples and reflections...

Dr. Manschoff had answered his questions well, yet new questions had arisen.

Most people didn't go crazy any more, the doctor had explained, and so there were very few treatment centers such as this.

Question: Why were there any at all?

A place like this cost a fortune to staff and maintain. In an age where living-space and areable acreage was at such a premium, why waste this vast and fertile expanse? And in a society more and more openly committed to the policy of promoting the greatest good for the greatest number, why bother about the fate of an admittedly insignificant group of mentally disturbed patients?

Not that Harry resented his situation; in fact, it was almost too good to be true.

Question: Was it too good to be true?

Why, come to realize it, he'd seen less than a dozen other patients during his entire stay here! All of them were male, and all of them—apparently—were recovering from a condition somewhat similar to his own. At least, he'd recognized the same reticence and diffidence when it came to exchanging more than a perfunctory greeting in an encounter in an outer corridor. At the time, he'd accepted their unwillingness to communicate; welcomed and understood it because of *his* condition. And that in itself wasn't what he questioned now.

But why were there so *few* patients beside himself? Why were they all males? And why weren't *they* roaming the countryside now the way he was?

So many staff-members and so few patients. So much room and luxury and freedom, and so little use of it. So little apparent purpose to it all.

Question: Was there a hidden purpose?

Harry stared down into the ripples and reflections, and the sun was suddenly intolerably hot, its glare on the water suddenly blinding and bewildering. He saw his face mirrored on the water's surface, and it was not the familiar countenance he knew—the features were bloated, distorted, shimmering and wavering.

Maybe it was starting all over again. Maybe he was getting another one of those headaches. Maybe he was going to lose control again.

Yes, and maybe he was just imagining things. Sitting here in all this heat wasn't a good idea.

Why not take a swim?

That seemed reasonable enough. In fact, it seemed like a delightful distraction. Harry rose and stripped. He entered the water awkwardly—one didn't dive, not after twenty years of abstinence from the outdoor life—but he found that he could swim, after a fashion. The water was cooling, soothing. A few minutes of immersion and Harry found himself forgetting his speculations. The uneasy feeling had vanished. Now, when he stared down into the water, he saw his own face reflected, looking just the way it should. And when he stared up—

He saw her standing there, on the bank.

She was tall, slim, and blonde. Very tall, very slim, and very blonde.

She was also very desirable.

Up until a moment ago, Harry had considered swimming a delightful distraction. But now—

"How's the water?" she called.

"Fine."

She nodded, smiling down at him.

"Aren't you coming in?" he asked.

"No."

"Then what are you doing here?"

"I was looking for you, Harry."

"You know my name?"

She nodded again. "Dr. Manschoff told me."

"You mean, he sent you here to find me?"

"That's right."

"But I don't understand. If you're not going swimming, then why—I mean—"

Her smile broadened. "It's just part of the therapy, Harry."

"Part of the therapy?"

"That's right. *Part.*" She giggled. "Don't you think you'd like to come out of the water now and see what the rest of it might be?"

Harry thought so.

With mounting enthusiasm, he eagerly embraced his treatment and entered into a state of active cooperation.

It was some time before he ventured to comment on the situation. "Manschoff is a damned good diagnostician," he murmured. Then he sat up. "Are you a patient here?"

She shook her head. "Don't ask questions, Harry. Can't you be satisfied with things as they are?"

"You're just what the doctor ordered, all right." He gazed down at her. "But don't you even have a name?"

"You can call me Sue."

"Thank you."

He bent to kiss her but she avoided him and rose to her feet. "Got to go now."

"So soon?"

She nodded and moved towards the bushes above the bank.

"But when will I see you again?"

"Coming swimming tomorrow?"

"Yes."

"Maybe I can get away for more occupational therapy then."

She stooped behind the bushes, and Harry saw a flash of white.

"You *are* a nurse, aren't you," he muttered. "On the staff, I suppose. I should have known."

"All right, so I am. What's that got to do with it?"

"And I suppose you were telling the truth when you said Manschoff sent you here. This *is* just part of my therapy, isn't it?"

She nodded briefly as she slipped into her uniform. "Does that bother you, Harry?"

He bit his lip. When he spoke, his voice was low. "Yes, damn it, it does. I mean, I got the idea—at least, I was hoping—that this wasn't just a matter of carrying out an assignment on your part."

She looked up at him gravely. "Who said anything about an assignment, darling?" she murmured. "I volunteered."

And then she was gone.

Then she was gone, and then she came back that night in Harry's dreams, and then she was at the river the next day and it was better than the dreams, better than the day before.

Sue told him she had been watching him for weeks now. And she had gone to Manschoff and suggested it, and she was very glad. And they had to meet here, out in the open, so as not to complicate the situation or disturb any of the other patients.

So Harry naturally asked her about the other patients, and the whole general setup, and she said Dr. Manschoff would answer all those questions in due time. But right now, with only an hour or so to spare, was he going to spend it all asking for information? Matters were accordingly adjusted to their mutual satisfaction, and it was on that basis that they continued their almost daily meetings for some time.

The next few months were perhaps the happiest Harry had ever known. The whole interval took on a dreamlike quality—idealized, romanticized, yet basically sensual. There is probably such a dream buried deep within the psyche of every man, Harry reflected, but to few is it ever given to realize its reality. His early questioning attitude gave way to a mood of mere acceptance and enjoyment. This was the primitive drama, the very essence of the male-female relationship; Adam and Eve in the Garden. Why waste time seeking the Tree of Knowledge?

And it wasn't until summer passed that Harry even thought about the Serpent.

One afternoon, as he sat waiting for Sue on the river bank, he heard a sudden movement in the brush behind him.

"Darling?" he called, eagerly.

"Please, you don't know me *that* well." The deep masculine voice carried overtones of amusement.

Flushing, Harry turned to confront the intruder. He was a short, stocky, middle-aged man whose bristling gray crewcut almost matched the neutral shades of his gray orderly's uniform.

"Expecting someone else, were you?" the man muttered. "Well, I'll get out of your way."

"That's not necessary. I was really just daydreaming, I guess. I don't know what made me think—" Harry felt his flush deepen, and he lowered his eyes and his voice as he tried to improvise some excuse.

"You're a lousy liar," the man said, stepping forward and seating himself on the bank next to Harry. "But it doesn't really matter. I don't think your girl friend is going to show up today, anyway."

"What do you mean? What do you know about—"

"I mean just what I said," the man told him. "And I know everything I need to know, about you and about her and about the situation in general. That's why I'm here, Collins."

He paused, watching the play of emotions in Harry's eyes.

"I know what you're thinking right now," the gray-haired man continued. "At first you wondered how I knew your name. Then you realized that if I was on the staff in the wards I'd naturally be able to identify the patients. Now it occurs to you that you've never seen me in the wards, so you're speculating as to whether or not I'm working out of the administration offices with that psychiatric no good Manschoff. But if I were, I wouldn't be calling him names, would I? Which means you're really getting confused, aren't you, Collins? Good!"

The man chuckled, but there was neither mockery, malice, nor genuine mirth in the sound. And his eyes were sober, intent.

"Who are you?" Harry asked. "What are you doing here?"

"The name is Ritchie, Arnold Ritchie. At least, that's the name they know me by around here, and you can call me that. As to what I'm doing, it's a long story. Let's just say that right now I'm here to give you a little advanced therapy."

"Then Manschoff did send you?"

The chuckle came again, and Ritchie shook his head. "He did not. And if he even suspected I was here, there'd be hell to pay."

"Then what do you want with me?"

"It isn't a question of what I want. It's a question of what *you need.* Which is, like I said, advanced therapy. The sort that dear old kindly permissive Father-Image Manschoff doesn't intend you to get."

Harry stood up. "What's this all about?"

Ritchie rose with him, smiling for the first time. "I'm glad you asked that question, Collins. It's about time you did, you know. Everything has been so carefully planned to keep you from asking it. But you *were* beginning to wonder just a bit anyway, weren't you?"

"I don't see what you're driving at."

"You don't see what anyone is driving at, Collins. You've been blinded by a spectacular display of kindness, misdirected by self-indulgence. I told you I knew everything I needed to know about you, and I do. Now I'm going to ask you to remember these things for yourself; the things you've avoided considering all this while.

"I'm going to ask you to remember that you're twenty-eight years old, and that for almost seven years you were an agency man and a good one. You worked hard, you did a conscientious job, you stayed in line, obeyed the rules, never rebelled. Am I correct in my summary of the situation?"

"Yes, I guess so."

"So what was your reward for all this unceasing effort and eternal conformity? A one-room apartment and a one-week vacation, once a year. Count your blessings, Collins. Am I right?"

"Right."

"Then what happened? Finally you flipped, didn't you? Tried to take a header out of the window. You chucked your job, chucked your responsibilities, chucked your future and attempted to chuck yourself away. Am I still right?"

"Yes."

"Good enough. And now we come to the interesting part of the story. Seven years of being a good little boy got you nothing but the promise of present and future frustration. Seven seconds of madness, of attempted self-destruction, brought you here. And as a reward for bucking the system, the system itself has provided you with a life of luxury and leisure—full permission to come and go as you please, live in spacious ease, indulge in the gratification of every appetite, free of responsibility or restraint. Is that true?"

"I suppose so."

"All right. Now, let me ask you the question you asked me. What's it all about?"

Ritchie put his hand on Harry's shoulder. "Tell me that, Collins. Why do you suppose you've received such treatment? As long as you stayed in line, nobody gave a damn for your comfort or welfare. Then, when you committed the cardinal sin of our present-day society—when you rebelled—everything was handed to you on a silver platter. Does that make sense?"

"But it's therapy. Dr. Manschoff said—"

"Look, Collins. Millions of people flip every year. Millions more attempt suicide. How many of them end up in a place like this?"

"They don't, though. That's just Naturalist propaganda. Dr. Manschoff said—"

"*Dr. Manschoff said!* I know what he said, all right. And you believed him, because you wanted to believe him. You wanted the reassurance he could offer you—the feeling of being unique and important. So you didn't ask him any questions, you didn't ask any questions of yourself. Such as why anybody would consider an insignificant little agency man, without friends, family or connections, worth the trouble of rehabilitating at all, let alone amidst such elaborate and expensive surroundings. Why, men like you are a dime a dozen these days—Vocational Apt can push a few buttons and come up with half a million replacements to take over your job. You aren't important to society, Collins. You aren't important to anyone at all, besides yourself. And yet you got the red-carpet treatment. It's about time somebody yanked that carpet out from under you. What's it all about?"

Harry blinked. "Look here, I don't see why this is any of your business. Besides, to tell the truth, I'm expecting—"

"I know who you're expecting, but I've already told you she won't be here. Because she's expecting."

"What—?"

"It's high time you learned the facts of life, Collins. Yes, the well-known facts of life—the ones about the birds and the bees, and barefoot boys and blondes, too. Your little friend Sue is going to have a souvenir."

"I don't believe it! I'm going to ask Dr. Manschoff."

"Sure you are. You'll ask Manschoff and he'll deny it. And so you'll tell him about me. You'll say you met somebody in the woods today—either a lunatic or a Naturalist spy who infiltrated here under false pretenses. And

Manschoff will reassure you. He'll reassure you just long enough to get his hands on me. Then he'll take care of both of us."

"Are you insinuating—"

"Hell, no! I'm *telling* you!" Ritchie put his hand down suddenly, and his voice calmed. "Ever wonder about those other two big buildings on the premises here, Collins? Well, I can tell you about one of them, because that's where I work. You might call it an experimental laboratory if you like. Sometime later on I'll describe it to you. But right now it's the other building that's important; the building with the big chimney. That's a kind of an incinerator, Collins—a place where the mistakes go up in smoke, at night, when there's nobody to see. A place where you and I will go up in smoke, if you're fool enough to tell Manschoff about this."

"You're lying."

"I wish to God I was, for both our sakes! But I can prove what I'm saying. *You* can prove it, for yourself."

"How?"

"Pretend this meeting never occurred. Pretend that you just spent the afternoon here, waiting for a girl who never showed up. Then do exactly what you would do under those circumstances. Go in to see Dr. Manschoff and ask him where Sue is, tell him you were worried because she'd promised to meet you and then didn't appear.

"I can tell you right now what he'll tell you. He'll say that Sue has been transferred to another treatment center, that she knew about it for several weeks but didn't want to upset you with the news of her departure. So she decided to just slip away. And Manschoff will tell you not to be unhappy. It just so happens that he knows of another nurse who has had her eye on you—a very pretty little brunette named Myrna. In fact, if you go down to the river tomorrow, you'll find her waiting for you there."

"What if I refuse?"

Ritchie shrugged. "Why should you refuse? It's all fun and games, isn't it? Up to now you haven't asked any questions about what was going on, and it would look very strange if you started at this late date. I strongly advise you to cooperate. If not, everything is likely to—quite literally—go up in smoke."

Harry Collins frowned. "All right, suppose I do what you say, and Manschoff gives me the answers you predict. This still doesn't prove that he'd be lying or that you're telling me the truth."

"Wouldn't it indicate as much, though?"

"Perhaps. But on the other hand, it could merely mean that you know Sue *has* been transferred, and that Dr. Manschoff intends to turn me over to a substitute. It doesn't necessarily imply anything sinister."

"In other words, you're insisting on a clincher, is that it?"

"Yes."

"All right." Ritchie sighed heavily. "You asked for it." He reached into the left-hand upper pocket of the gray uniform and brought out a small, stiff square of glossy paper.

"What's that?" Harry asked. He reached for the paper, but Ritchie drew his hand back.

"Look at it over my shoulder," he said. "I don't want any fingerprints. Hell of a risky business just smuggling it out of the files—no telling how well they check up on this material."

Harry circled behind the smaller man. He squinted down. "Hard to read."

"Sure. It's a photostat. I made it myself, this morning; that's my department. Read carefully now. You'll see it's a transcript of the lab report. Susan Pulver, that's her name, isn't it? After due examination and upon completion of preliminary tests, hereby found to be in the second month of pregnancy. Putative father, Harry Collins—that's you, see your name? And here's the rest of the record."

"Yes, let me see it. What's all this about inoculation series? And who is this Dr. Leffingwell?" Harry bent closer, but Ritchie closed his hand around the photostat and pocketed it again.

"Never mind that, now. I'll tell you later. The important thing is, do you believe me?"

"I believe Sue is pregnant, yes."

"That's enough. Enough for you to do what I've asked you to. Go to Manschoff and make inquiries. See what he tells you. Don't make a scene, and for God's sake don't mention my name. Just confirm my story for yourself. Then I'll give you further details."

"But when will I see you?"

"Tomorrow afternoon, if you like. Right here."

"You said he'd be sending another girl—"

Ritchie nodded. "So I did. And so he'll say. I suggest you beg to be excused for the moment. Tell him it will take a while for you to get over the shock of losing Sue this way."

"I won't be lying," Harry murmured.

"I know. And I'm sorry. Believe me, I am." Ritchie sighed again. "But you'll just have to trust me from now on."

"Trust you? When you haven't even explained what this is all about?"

"You've had your shock-therapy for today. Come back for another treatment tomorrow."

And then Ritchie was gone, the gray uniform melting away into the gray shadows of the shrubbery above the bank.

A short time later, Harry made his own way back to the center in the gathering twilight. The dusk was gray, too. Everything seemed gray now.

So was Harry Collins' face, when he emerged from his interview with Dr. Manschoff that evening. And it was still pallid the next afternoon when he came down to the river bank and waited for Ritchie to reappear.

The little man emerged from the bushes. He stared at Harry's drawn countenance and nodded slowly.

"I was right, eh?" he muttered.

"It looks that way. But I can't understand what's going on. If this isn't just a treatment center, if they're not really interested in my welfare, then what am I doing here?"

"You're taking part in an experiment. This, my friend, is a laboratory. And you are a nice, healthy guinea pig."

"But that doesn't make sense. I haven't been experimented on. They've let me do as I please."

"Exactly. And what do guinea pigs excel at? *Breeding.*"

"You mean this whole thing was rigged up just so that Sue and I would—?"

"Please, let's not be so egocentric, shall we? After all, you're not the *only* male patient in this place. There are a dozen others wandering around loose. Some of them have their favorite caves, others have discovered little bypaths, but all of them seem to have located ideal trysting-places. Whereupon, of course, the volunteer nurses have located *them.*"

"Are you telling me the same situation exists with each of the others?"

"Isn't it fairly obvious? You've shown no inclination to become friendly with the rest of the patients here, and none of them have made any overtures to you. That's because everyone has his own little secret, his own private arrangement. And so all of you go around fooling everybody else, and all of you are being fooled. I'll give credit to Manschoff and his staff on that point—he's certainly mastered the principles of practical psychology."

"But you talked about breeding. With our present overpopulation problem, why in the world do they deliberately encourage the birth of more children?"

"Very well put. 'Why in the world' indeed! In order to answer that, you'd better take a good look at the world."

Arnold Ritchie seated himself on the grass, pulled out a pipe, and then replaced it hastily. "Better not smoke," he murmured. "Be awkward if we attracted any attention and were found together."

Harry stared at him. "You *are* a Naturalist, aren't you?"

"I'm a reporter, by profession."

"Which network?"

"No network. *Newzines.* There are still a few in print, you know."

"I know. But I can't afford them."

"There aren't many left who can, or who even feel the need of reading them. Nevertheless, mavericks like myself still cling to the ancient and honorable practices of the Fourth Estate. One of which is ferreting out the inside story, the news behind the news."

"Then you're not working for the Naturalists."

"Of course I am. I'm working for them and for everybody else who has an interest in learning the truth." Ritchie paused. "By the way, you keep using that term as if it were some kind of dirty word. Just what does it mean? What *is* a Naturalist, in your book?"

"Why, a radical thinker, of course. An opponent of government policies, of progress. One who believes we're running out of living space, using up the last of our natural resources."

"What do you suppose motivates Naturalists, really?"

"Well, they can't stand the pressures of daily living, or the prospects of a future when we'll be still more hemmed in."

Ritchie nodded. "Any more than you could, a few months ago, when you tried to commit suicide. Wouldn't you say that *you* were thinking like a Naturalist then?"

Harry grimaced. "I suppose so."

"Don't feel ashamed. You saw the situation clearly, just as the so-called Naturalists do. And just as the government does. Only the government can't dare admit it—hence the secrecy behind this project."

"A hush-hush government plan to stimulate further breeding? I still don't see—"

"Look at the world," Ritchie repeated. "Look at it realistically. What's the situation at present? Population close to six billion, and rising fast. There was a leveling-off period in the Sixties, and then it started to climb again. No wars, no disease to cut it down. The development of synthetic foods, the use of algae and fungi, rules out famine as a limiting factor. Increased harnessing of atomic power has done away with widespread poverty, so there's no economic deterrent to propagation. Neither church nor state dares set up a legal prohibition. So here we are, at the millennium. In place of international tension we've substituted internal tension. In place of thermonuclear explosion, we have a population explosion."

"You make it look pretty grim."

"I'm just talking about today. What happens ten years from now, when we hit a population-level of ten billion? What happens when we reach twenty billion, fifty billion, a hundred? Don't talk to me about more substitutes, more synthetics, new ways of conserving top-soil. There just isn't going to be *room* for everyone!"

"Then what's the answer?"

"That's what the government wants to know. Believe me, they've done a lot of searching; most of it *sub rosa*. And then along came this man Leffingwell, with *his* solution. That's just what it is, of course—an endocrinological solution, for direct injection."

"Leffingwell? The Dr. Leffingwell whose name was on that photostat? What's he got to do with all this?"

"He's boss of this project," Ritchie said. "He's the one who persuaded them to set up a breeding-center. You're *his* guinea pig."

"But why all the secrecy?"

"That's what I wanted to know. That's why I scurried around, pulled strings to get a lab technician's job here. It wasn't easy, believe me. The whole deal is being kept strictly under wraps until Leffingwell's experiments prove out. They realized right away that it would be fatal to use volunteers for the experiments—they'd be bound to talk, there'd be leaks. And of course, they anticipated some awkward results at first, until the technique is refined and perfected. Well, they were right on that score. I've seen some of their failures." Ritchie shuddered. "Any volunteer—any military man, government employee or even a so-called dedicated scientist who broke away would spread enough rumors about what was going on to kill the entire project. That's why they decided to use mental patients for subjects. God knows, they had millions to choose from, but they were very particular. You're a rare specimen, Collins."

"How so?"

"Because you happen to fit all their specifications. You're young, in good physical condition. Unlike ninety percent of the population, you don't even wear contact lenses, do you? And your aberration was temporary, easily removed by removing you from the tension-sources which created it. You have no family ties, no close friends, to question your absence. That's why you were chosen—one of the two hundred."

"Two hundred? But there's only a dozen others here now."

"A dozen males, yes. You're forgetting the females. Must be about fifty or sixty in the other building."

"But if you're talking about someone like Sue, she's a nurse—"

Ritchie shook his head. "That's what she was *told* to say. Actually, she's a patient, too. They're all patients. Twelve men and sixty women, at the moment. Originally, about thirty men and a hundred and seventy women."

"What happened to the others?"

"I told you there were some failures. Many of the women died in childbirth. Some of them survived, but found out about the results—and the results, up until now, haven't been perfect. A few of the men found out, too. Well, they have only one method of dealing with failures here. They dispose of them. I told you about that chimney, didn't I?"

"You mean they killed the offspring, killed those who found out about them?"

Ritchie shrugged.

"But what are they actually *doing*? Who is this Dr. Leffingwell? What's it all about?"

"I think I can answer those questions for you."

Harry wheeled at the sound of the familiar voice.

Dr. Manschoff beamed down at him from the top of the river bank. "Don't be alarmed," he said. "I wasn't following you with any intent to eavesdrop. I was merely concerned about him." His eyes flickered as he directed his gaze past Harry's shoulder, and Harry turned again to look at Arnold Ritchie.

The little man was no longer standing and he was no longer alone. Two attendants now supported him, one on either side, and Ritchie himself sagged against their grip with eyes closed. A hypodermic needle in one attendant's hand indicated the reason for Ritchie's sudden collapse.

"Merely a heavy sedative," Dr. Manschoff murmured. "We came prepared, in expectation of just such an emergency." He nodded at his companions. "Better take him back now," he said. "I'll look in on him this evening, when he comes out of it."

"Sorry about all this," Manschoff continued, sitting down next to Harry as the orderlies lifted Ritchie's inert form and carried him up the slanting slope. "It's entirely my fault. I misjudged my patient—never should have permitted him such a degree of freedom. Obviously, he's not ready for it yet. I do hope he didn't upset you in any way."

"No. He seemed quite"—Harry hesitated, then went on hastily—"logical."

"Indeed he is." Dr. Manschoff smiled. "Paranoid delusions, as they used to call them, can often be rationalized most convincingly. And from what little I heard, he was doing an excellent job, wasn't he?"

"Well—"

"I know." A slight sigh erased the smile. "Leffingwell and I are mad scientists, conducting biological experiments on human guinea pigs. We've assembled patients for breeding purposes and the government is secretly subsidizing us. Also, we incinerate our victims—again, with full governmental permission. All very logical, isn't it?"

"I didn't mean that," Harry told him. "It's just that he said Sue was pregnant and he was hinting things."

"Said?" Manschoff stood up. "*Hinted?* I'm surprised he didn't go further than that. Just today, we discovered he'd been using the office facilities—he had a sort of probationary position, as you may have guessed, helping out the staff in administration—to provide tangible proof of his artistic creations. He was writing out 'official reports' and then photostating them. Apparently he intended to circulate the results as 'evidence' to support his delusions. Look, here's a sample."

Dr. Manschoff passed a square of glossy paper to Harry, who scanned it quickly. It was another laboratory report similar to the one Ritchie had shown him, but containing a different set of names.

"No telling how long this sort of thing has been going on," Manschoff said. "He may have made dozens. Naturally, the moment we discovered it, we realized prompt action was necessary. He'll need special attention."

"But what's wrong with him?"

"It's a long story. He was a reporter at one time—he may have told you that. The death of his wife precipitated a severe trauma and brought him to our attention. Actually, I'm not at liberty to say any more regarding his case; you understand, I'm sure."

"Then you're telling me that everything he had to say was a product of his imagination?"

"No, don't misunderstand. It would be more correct to state that he merely distorted reality. For example, there *is* a Dr. Leffingwell on the staff here; he is a diagnostician and has nothing to do with psychotherapy *per se*. And he has charge of the hospital ward in Unit Three, the third building you may have noticed behind Administration. That's where the nurses maintain residence, of course. Incidentally, when any nurses take on a—special assignment, as it were, such as yours, Leffingwell does examine and treat them. There's a new oral contraception technique he's evolved which may be quite efficacious. But I'd hardly call it an example of sinister experimentation under the circumstances, would you?"

Harry shook his head. "About Ritchie, though," he said. "What will happen to him?"

"I can't offer any prognosis. In view of my recent error in judgment concerning him, it's hard to say how he'll respond to further treatment. But rest assured that I'll do my best for his case. Chances are you'll be seeing him again before very long."

Dr. Manschoff glanced at his watch. "Shall we go back now?" he suggested. "Supper will be served soon."

The two men toiled up the bank.

Harry discovered that the doctor was right about supper. It was being served as he returned to his room. But the predictions concerning Ritchie didn't work out quite as well.

It was after supper—indeed, quite some hours afterwards, while Harry sat at his window and stared sleeplessly out into the night—that he noted the thick, greasy spirals of black smoke rising suddenly from the chimney of the Third Unit building. And the sight may have prepared him for the failure of Dr. Manschoff's prophecy regarding his disturbed patient.

Harry never asked any questions, and no explanations were ever forthcoming.

But from that evening onward, nobody ever saw Arnold Ritchie again.

CHAPTER THREE
President Winthrop—1999

The Secretary of State closed the door.

"Well?" he asked.

President Winthrop looked up from the desk and blinked. "Hello, Art," he said. "Sit down."

"Sorry I'm late," the Secretary told him. "I came as soon as I got the call."

"It doesn't matter." The President lit a cigarette and pursed his lips around it until it stopped wobbling. "I've been checking the reports all night."

"You look tired."

"I am. I could sleep for a week. That is, I *wish* I could."

"Any luck?"

The President pushed the papers aside and drummed the desk for a moment. Then he offered the Secretary a gray ghost of a smile.

"The answer's still the same."

"But this was our last chance—"

"I know." The President leaned back. "When I think of the time and effort, the money that's been poured into these projects! To say nothing of the hopes we had. And now, it's all for nothing."

"You can't say that," the Secretary answered. "After all, we did reach the moon. We got to Mars." He paused. "No one can take that away from you. You sponsored the Martian flights. You fought for the appropriations, pushed the project, carried it through. You helped mankind realize its greatest dream—"

"Save that for the newscasts," the President said. "The fact remains, we've succeeded. And our success was a failure. Mankind's greatest dream, eh? Read these reports and you'll find out this is mankind's greatest nightmare."

"Is it that bad?"

"Yes." The President slumped in his chair. "It's that bad. We can reach the moon at will. Now we can send a manned flight to Mars. But it means nothing. We can't support life in either place. There's absolutely no possibility of establishing or maintaining an outpost, let alone a large colony or a permanent human residence. That's what all the reports conclusively demonstrate.

"Every bit of oxygen, every bit of food and clothing and material, would have to be supplied. And investigations prove there's no chance of ever realizing any return. The cost of such an operation is staggeringly prohibitive. Even if there was evidence to show it might be possible to undertake some mining projects, it wouldn't begin to defray expenses, once you consider the transportation factor."

"But if they improve the rockets, manage to make room for a bigger payload, wouldn't it be cheaper?"

"It would still cost roughly a billion dollars to equip a flight and maintain a personnel of twenty men for a year," the President told him. "I've checked into that, and even this estimate is based on the most optimistic projection. So you can see there's no use in continuing now. We'll never solve our problems by attempting to colonize the moon or Mars."

"But it's the only possible solution left to us."

"No it isn't," the President said. "There's always our friend Leffingwell."

The Secretary of State turned away. "You can't officially sponsor a thing like that," he muttered. "It's political suicide."

The gray smile returned to the gray lips. "Suicide? What do you know about suicide, Art? I've been reading a few statistics on *that*, too. How many actual suicides do you think we had in this country last year?"

"A hundred thousand? Two hundred, maybe?"

"Two million." The President leaned forward. "Add to that, over a million murders and six million crimes of violence."

"I never knew—"

"Damned right you didn't! We used to have a Federal Bureau of Investigation to help prevent such things. Now the big job is merely to hush them up. We're doing everything in our power just to keep these matters quiet, or else there'd be utter panic. Then there's the accident total and the psycho rate. We can't build institutions fast enough to hold the mental cases, nor train doctors enough to care for them. Shifting them into other jobs in other areas doesn't cure, and it no longer even disguises what is happening. At this rate, another ten years will see half the nation going insane. And it's like this all over the world.

"This is race-suicide, Art. Race-suicide through sheer fecundity. Leffingwell is right. The reproductive instinct, unchecked, will overbalance group survival in the end. How long has it been since you were out on the streets?"

The Secretary of State shrugged. "You know I never go out on the streets," he said. "It isn't very safe."

"Of course not. But it's no safer for the hundreds of millions who have to go out every day. Accident, crime, the sheer maddening proximity of the crowds—these phenomena are increasing through mathematical progression. And they must be stopped. Leffingwell has the only answer."

"They won't buy it," warned the Secretary. "Congress won't, and the voters won't, any more than they bought birth-control. And this is worse."

"I know that, too." The President rose and walked over to the window, looking out at the sky-scraper apartments which loomed across what had once been the Mall. He was trying to find the dwarfed spire of Washington's Monument in the tangled maze of stone.

"If I go before the people and sponsor Leffingwell, I'm through. Through as President, through with the Party. They'll crucify me. But somebody in authority must push this project. That's the beginning. Once it's known, people will have to think about the possibilities. There'll be opposition, then controversy, then debate. And gradually Leffingwell will gain adherents. It may take five years, it may take ten.

Finally, the change will come. First through volunteers. Then by law. I only pray that it happens soon."

"They'll curse your name," the Secretary said. "They'll try to kill you. It's going to be hell."

"Hell for me if I do, yes. Worse hell for the whole world if I don't."

"But are you quite sure it will work? His method, I mean?"

"You saw the reports on his tests, didn't you? It works, all right. We've got more than just abstract data, now. We've got films for the telescreenings all set up."

"Films? You mean you'll actually *show* what the results are? Why, just telling the people will be bad enough. And admitting the government sponsored the project under wraps. But when they *see*, nothing on earth can save you from assassination."

"Perhaps. It doesn't really matter." The President crushed his cigarette in the ashtray. "One less mouth to feed. And I'm getting pretty sick of synthetic meals, anyway."

President Winthrop turned to the Secretary, his eyes brightening momentarily. "Tell you what, Art. I'm not planning on breaking the proposal to the public until next Monday. What say we have a little private dinner party on Saturday evening, just the Cabinet members and their wives? Sort of a farewell celebration, in a way, but we won't call it that, of course? Chef tells me there's still twenty pounds of hamburger in the freezers."

"Twenty pounds of hamburger? You mean it?" The Secretary of State was smiling, too.

"That's right." The President of the United States grinned in anticipation. "Been a long time since I've tasted a real, honest-to-goodness hamburger."

CHAPTER FOUR
Harry Collins—2000

Harry didn't ask any questions. He just kept his mouth shut and waited. Maybe Dr. Manschoff suspected and maybe he didn't. Anyway, there was no trouble. Harry figured there wouldn't be, as long as he stayed in line and went through the proper motions. It was all a matter of pretending to conform, pretending to agree, pretending to believe.

So he watched his step—*except in the dreams, and then he was always falling into the yawning abyss.*

He kept his nose clean—*but in the dreams he smelled the blood and brimstone of the pit.*

He managed to retain a cheerful smile at all times—*though, in the dreams, he screamed.*

Eventually, he even met Myrna. She was the pretty little brunette whom Ritchie had mentioned, and she did her best to console him—*only in dreams, when he embraced her, he was embracing a writhing coil of slimy smoke.*

It may have been that Harry Collins went a little mad, just having to pretend that he was sane. But he learned the way, and he managed. He saved the madness *(or was it the reality?)* for the dreams.

Meanwhile he waited and said nothing.

He said nothing when, after three months or so, Myrna was suddenly "transferred" without warning.

He said nothing when, once a week or so, he went in to visit with Dr. Manschoff.

He said nothing when Manschoff volunteered the information that Ritchie had been "transferred" too, or suggested that it would be best to stay on for "further therapy."

And he said nothing when still a third nurse came his way; a woman who was callid, complaisant, and nauseatingly nymphomaniac.

The important thing was to stay alive. Stay alive and try to learn.

It took him almost an additional year to find out what he wanted to find out. More than eight months passed before he found a way of sneaking out of his room at night, and a way of getting into that Third Unit through a delivery door which was occasionally left open through negligence.

Even then, all he learned was that the female patients did have their living quarters here, along with the members of the staff and—presumably—Dr. Leffingwell. Many of the women *were* patients rather than nurses, as claimed, and a good number of them were in various stages of pregnancy, but this proved nothing.

Several times Harry debated the possibilities of taking some of the other men in his Unit into his confidence. Then he remembered what had happened to Arnold Ritchie and decided against this course. The risk was too great. He had to continue alone.

It wasn't until Harry managed to get into Unit Four that he got what he wanted (what he *didn't* want) and learned that reality and dreams were one and the same.

There was the night, more than a year after he'd come to the treatment center, when he finally broke into the basement and found the incinerators. And the incinerators led to the operating and delivery chambers, and the delivery chambers led to the laboratory and the laboratory led to the incubators and the incubators led to the nightmare.

In the nightmare Harry found himself looking down at the mistakes and the failures and he recognized them for what they were, and he knew then why the incinerators were kept busy and why the black smoke poured.

In the nightmare he saw the special units containing those which were not mistakes or failures, and in a way they were worse than the others. They were red and wriggling there beneath the glass, and on the glass surfaces hung the charts which gave the data. Then Harry saw the names, saw his own name repeated twice—once for Sue, once for Myrna. And he realized that he had contributed to the successful outcome or issue of the experiments (*outcome? Issue? These horrors?*) and that was why Manschoff must have chosen to take the risk of keeping him alive. Because he was one of the *good* guinea pigs, and he had spawned, spawned living, mewing abominations.

He had dreamed of these things, and now he saw that they were real, so that nightmare merged with *now*, and he could gaze down at it with open eyes and scream at last with open mouth.

Then, of course, an attendant came running (*although he seemed to be moving ever so slowly, because everything moves so slowly in a dream*) and Harry saw him coming and lifted a bell-glass and smashed it down over the man's head (*slowly, ever so slowly*) and then he heard the others coming and he climbed out of the window and ran.

The searchlights winked across the courtyards and the sirens vomited hysteria from metallic throats and the night was filled with shadows that pursued.

But Harry knew where to run. He ran straight through the nightmare, through all the fantastic but familiar convolutions of sight and sound, and then he came to the river and plunged in.

Now the nightmare was not sight or sound, but merely sensation. Icy cold and distilled darkness; ripples that ran, then raced and roiled and roared. But there had to be a way out of the nightmare and there had to be a way out of the canyon, and that way was the river.

Apparently no one else had thought of the river; perhaps they had considered it as a possible avenue of escape and then discarded the notion when they realized how it ripped and raged among the rocks as it finally plunged from the canyon's mouth. Obviously, no one could hope to combat that current and survive.

But strange things happen in nightmares. And you fight the numbness and the blackness and you claw and convulse and you twist and turn and toss and then you ride the crests of frenzy and plunge into the troughs of panic and despair and you sweep round and round and sink down into nothingness until you break through to the freedom which comes only with oblivion.

Somewhere beyond the canyon's moiling maw, Harry Collins found that freedom and that oblivion. He escaped from the nightmare, just as he escaped from the river.

The river itself roared on without him.

And the nightmare continued, too...

CHAPTER FIVE
Minnie Schultz—2009

When Frank came home, Minnie met him at the door. She didn't say a word, just handed him the envelope containing the notice.

"What's the matter?" Frank asked, trying to take her in his arms. "You been crying."

"Never mind." Minnie freed herself. "Just read what it says there."

Frank read slowly, determinedly, his features contorted in concentration. Vocational Apt had terminated his schooling at the old grade-school level, and while like all students he had been taught enough so that he could read the necessary advertising commercials, any printed message of this sort provided a definite challenge.

Halfway through the notice he started to scowl. "What kind of monkey business is this?"

"No monkey business. It's the new law. Everybody that gets married in Angelisco takes the shots, from now on. Fella from State Hall, he told me when he delivered this."

"We'll see about this," Frank muttered. "No damn government's gonna tell me how to run my life. Sa free country, ain't so?"

Minnie's mouth began to twitch. "They're coming back tomorra morning, the fella said. To give me the first shots. Gee, honey, I'm scared, like. I don't want 'em."

"That settles it," Frank said. "We're getting out of this place, fast."

"Where'd we go?"

"Dunno. Someplace. Texas, maybe. I was listening to the 'casts at work today. They don't have this law in Texas. Not yet, anyway. Come on, start packing."

"Packing? But how'll we get there?"

"Fly. We'll jet right out."

"You got prior'ty reservations or something?"

"No." The scowl returned to Frank's forehead. "But maybe if I pitch 'em a sob story, tell 'em it's our honeymoon, you know, then we could—"

Minnie shook her head. "It won't work, honey. You know that. Takes six months to get a prior'ty clearance or whatever they call it. Besides, your job and all—what'll you do in Texas? They've got your number listed here. Why, we couldn't even *land*, like. I bet Texas is even more crowded than Angelisco these days, in the cities. And all the rest of it is Ag Culture project, isn't it?"

Frank was leaning against the sink, listening. Now he took three steps forward and sat down on the bed. He didn't look at her as he spoke.

"Well, we gotta do something," he said. "You don't want those shots and that's for sure. Maybe I can have one of those other things instead, those whaddya-call-'ems."

"You mean where they operate you, like?"

"That's right. A vas-something. You know, sterilize you. Then we won't have to worry."

Minnie took a deep breath. Then she sat down and put her arm around Frank.

"But you wanted kids," she murmured. "You told me, when we got married, you always wanted to have a son—"

Frank pulled away.

"Sure I do," he said. "A son. That's what I want. A *real* son. Not a freak. Not a damned little monster that has to go to the Clinic every month and take injections so it won't grow. And what happens to you if you take *your* shots now? What if they drive you crazy or something?"

Minnie put her arm around Frank again and made him look at her. "That's not true," she told him. "That's just a lot of Naturalist talk. I know."

"Hell you do."

"But I do, honey! Honest, like! May Stebbins, she took the shots last year, when they asked for volunteers. And she's all right. You seen her baby yourself, remember? It's the sweetest little thing, and awful smart! So maybe it wouldn't be so bad."

"I'll ask about being operated tomorrow," Frank said. "Forget it. It don't matter."

"Of course it matters." Minnie looked straight at him. "Don't you think I know what you been going through? Sweating it out on that job day after day, going nuts in the traffic, saving up the ration coupons so's we'd have extra food for the honeymoon and all?

"You didn't have to marry me, you know that. It was just like we could have a place of our own together, and kids. Well, we're gonna have 'em, honey. I'll take the shots."

Frank shook his head but said nothing.

"It won't be so bad," Minnie went on. "The shots don't hurt at all, and they make it easier, carrying the baby. They say you don't even get morning sickness or anything. And just think, when we have a kid, we get a chance for a bigger place. We go right on the housing lists. We can have two rooms. A real bedroom, maybe."

Frank stared at her. "Is that all you can think about?" he asked. "A real bedroom?"

"But honey—"

"What about the kid?" he muttered. "How you suppose it's gonna feel? How'd you like to grow up and *not* grow up? How'd you like to be a midget three feet high in a world where everybody else is bigger? What kind of a life you call *that*? I want my son to have a decent chance."

"He will have."

Minnie stared back at him, but she wasn't seeing his face. "Don't you understand, honey? This isn't just something happening to *us*. We're not special. It's happening to everybody, all over the country, all over the world. You seen it in the 'casts, haven't you? Most states, they adopted the laws. And in a couple more years it'll be the only way anyone will ever have kids. Ten, twenty years from now, the kids will be growing up. Ours won't be different then, because from now on all the kids will be just like he is. The same size."

"I thought you was afraid of the shots," Frank said.

Minnie was still staring. "I was, honey. Only, I dunno. I keep thinking about Grandma."

"What's the old lady got to do with it?"

"Well, I remember when I was a little girl, like. How my Grandma always used to tell me about *her* Grandma, when *she* was a little girl.

"She was saying about how in the old days, before there even was an Angelisco—when her Grandma came out here in a covered wagon. Just think, honey, she was younger than I am, and she come thousands and thousands of miles in a wagon! With real horses, like! Wasn't any houses, no people or nothing. Except Indians that shot at them. And they climbed up the mountains and they crossed over the deserts and went hungry and thirsty and had fights with those Indians all the way. But they never stopped until they got here. Because they was the pioneers."

"Pioneers?"

"That's what Grandma said *her* Grandma called herself. A pioneer. She was real proud of it, too. Because it means having the courage to cut loose from all the old things and try something new when you need to. Start a whole new world, a whole new kind of life."

She sighed. "I always wanted to be a pioneer, like, but I never thought I'd get the chance."

"What are you talking about? What's all this got to do with us, or having a kid?"

"Don't you see? Taking these shots, having a baby this new way—it's sort of being a pioneer, too. Gonna help bring a new kind of people into a new kind of world. And if that's not being a pioneer, like, it's the closest I can come to it. It sounds right to me now."

Minnie smiled and nodded. "I guess I made up my mind just now. I'm taking the shots."

"Hell you are!" Frank told her. "We'll talk about it some more in the morning."

But Minnie continued to smile.

And that night, as she lay in the utility bed, the squeaking of the springs became the sound of turning wheels. The plastic walls and ceiling of the eightieth-floor apartment turned to billowing canvas, and the thunder of the passing jets transformed itself into the drumming hoofbeats of a million buffalo.

Let Frank talk to her again in the morning if he liked, Minnie thought. It wouldn't make any difference now. Because you can't stop us pioneers.

CHAPTER SIX
Harry Collins—2012

Harry crouched behind the boulders, propping the rifle up between the rocks, and adjusted the telescopic sights. The distant doorway sprang into sharp focus. Grunting with satisfaction, he settled down to his vigil. The rifle-barrel had been dulled down against detection by reflection, and Harry's dark glasses protected him against the glare of the morning sun. He might have to wait several hours now, but he didn't care. It had taken him twelve years to come this far, and he was willing to wait a little while longer.

Twelve years. Was it really that long?

A mirror might have answered him; a mirror might have shown him the harsh features of a man of forty-two. But Harry needed no mirror. He could remember the past dozen years only too easily—though they had not been easy years.

Surviving the river was only the beginning. Animal strength carried him through that ordeal. But he emerged from the river as an animal; a wounded animal, crawling through the brush and arroyo outside the southern Colorado canyon.

And it was animal cunning which preserved him. He'd wandered several days until he encountered Emil Grizek and his outfit. By that time he was half-starved and completely delirious. It took a month until he was up and around again.

But Emil and the boys had nursed him through. They took turns caring for him in the bunkhouse; their methods were crude but efficient and Harry was grateful. Best of all, they asked no questions. Harry's status was that of a hunted fugitive, without a Vocational Apt record or rating. The authorities or any prospective employers would inquire into these things, but Emil Grizek never seemed curious. By the time Harry was up and around again, he'd been accepted as one of the bunch. He told them his name was Harry Sanders, and that was enough.

Two months after they found him, he'd signed on with Emil Grizek and found a new role in life.

Harry Collins, advertising copywriter, had become Harry Sanders, working cowhand.

There was surprisingly little difficulty. Grizek had absentee employers who weren't interested in their foreman's methods, just as long as he recruited his own wranglers for the Bar B Ranch. Nobody demanded to see Apt cards or insisted on making out formal work-reports, and the pay was in cash. Cowhands were hard to come by these days, and it was an unspoken premise that the men taking on such jobs would be vagrants, migratory workers, fugitives from justice and injustice. A generation or so ago they might have become tramps—but the last of the hoboes had vanished along with the last of the freight trains. Once the derelicts haunted the canyons of the big cities; today there was no place for them there, so they fled to the canyons of the west. Harry had found himself a new niche, and no questions asked.

Oddly enough, he fitted in. The outdoor life agreed with him, and in a matter of months he was a passable cowpoke; within a year he was one of Grizek's top hands.

He learned to ride a bucking jeep with the best of them, and he could spot, single out, and stun a steer in forty seconds flat; then use his electronic brander on it and have the critter back on its feet in just under a minute.

Work was no problem, and neither was recreation. The bunkhouse offered crude but adequate facilities for living; old-fashioned air-conditioning and an antique infra-red broiler seemed good enough for roughing it, and Cookie at least turned out real man-sized meals. Eating genuine beef and honest-to-goodness baked bread was a treat, and so was having the luxury of all that space in the sleeping quarters. Harry thrived on it.

And some of the other hands were interesting companions. True, they were renegades and mavericks, but they were each of them unique and individual, and Harry enjoyed listening to them fan the breeze during the long nights.

There was Big Phil, who was pushing sixty now. But you'd never know it, not unless you got him to talking about the old days when he'd been a boy in Detroit. His daddy had been one of the last of the Union Men, back in the days of what they used to call the Organized Labor Movement. He could tell you about wage-hour agreements and the Railroad Brotherhood and contract negotiations almost as if he knew of these things through personal experience. He even remembered the Democratic Party. Phil got out when the government took over and set up Vocational Apt and Industrial Supervision; that's when he drifted west.

Tom Lowery's family had been military; he claimed to have been a member of the last graduating class ever to leave West Point. When the armament race ended, his prospects of a career vanished, and he settled down as a guard at Canaveral. Finally, he'd headed for the open country.

Bassett was the scholar of the outfit. He could sit around and quote old-time book-authors by the hour—classic writers like Prather and Spillane. In another age he might have been a college professor or even a football coach; he had an aptitude for the arts.

And there was Lobo, the misogynist, who had fled a wife and eleven children back in Monterey; and Januzki, who used to be mixed up with one of those odd religious cults out on the Coast. He bragged he'd been one of the Big Daddy-Os in the Beat Generationists, and he argued with Bassett about some old-time evangelist named Kerouac.

Best of all, though, Harry liked talking to Nick Kendrick. Nick's hobby was music, and he treasured his second-hand stereophonic unit and collection of tapes. He too was a classicist in his way, and there was many a long winter night when Harry sat there listening to ancient folk songs. The quaint atonalities of progressive jazz and the childishly frantic rhythms of "cool sounds" were somehow soothing and reassuring in their reminder of a simple heritage from a simpler age.

But above all, these men were wranglers, and they took a peculiar pride in the traditions of their own calling. There wasn't a one of them who wouldn't spend hours mulling over the lore of the range and the prairie. They knew the Great Names from the Great Days—Eugene Autry, Wyatt Earp, the legendary Thomas Mix, Dale Robertson, Paladin, and all the others; men who rode actual horses in the era when the West was really an untamed frontier.

And like the cowboys they were, they maintained the customs of other days. Every few months they rode a bucking helicopter into some raw western town—Las Vegas, or Reno, or even over to Palm Springs—to drink recklessly in the cocktail lounges, gamble wildly at the slots, or "go down the line" with some telescreen model on location for outdoor ad-backgrounds. There were still half a dozen such sin-cities scattered throughout the west; even the government acknowledged the need of lonely men to blow off steam. And though Ag Culture officially disapproved of the whole cowhand system, and talked grimly of setting up new and more efficient methods for training personnel and handling the cattle ranges, nothing was ever done. Perhaps the authorities knew that it was a hopeless task; only the outcasts and iconoclasts had the temperament necessary to survive such loneliness under an open sky. City-dwelling conformists just could not endure the monotony.

But even Emil Grizek's hands marvelled at the way Harry lived. He never joined them in their disorderly descent upon the scarlet cities of the plain, and most of the time he didn't even seem to watch the telescreen. If anything, he deliberately avoided all possible contact with civilization.

Since he never volunteered any information about his own past, they privately concluded that he was just a psychopathic personality.

"Strong regressive and seclusive tendencies," Bassett explained, solemnly.

"Sure," Nick Kendrick nodded, wisely. "You mean a Mouldy Fig, like."

"Creeping Meatball," muttered cultist Januzki. Not being religious fanatics, the others didn't understand the reference. But gradually they came to accept Harry's isolationist ways as the norm—at least, for him. And since he never quarreled, never exhibited any signs of dissatisfaction, he was left to his own pattern.

Thus it was all the more surprising when that pattern was rudely and abruptly shattered.

Harry remembered the occasion well. It was the day the Leff Law was officially upheld by the Supremist Courts. The whole business came over the telescreens and there was no way of avoiding it—you couldn't avoid it, because everybody was talking about it and everybody was watching.

"Now what do you think?" Emil Grizek demanded. "Any woman wants a baby, she's got to have those shots. They say kids shrink down into nothing. Weigh less than two pounds when they're born, and never grow up to be any bigger than midgets. You ask me, the whole thing's plumb loco, to say nothing of psychotic."

"I dunno." This from Big Phil. "Reckon they just about have to do something, the way cities are filling up and all. Tell me every spot in the country, except for the plains states here, is busting at the seams. Same in Europe, Africa, South America. Running out of space, running out of food, all over the world. This man Leffingwell figures on cutting down on size so's to keep the whole shebang going."

"But why couldn't it be done on a voluntary basis?" Bassett demanded. "These arbitrary rulings are bound to result in frustrations. And can you imagine what will happen to the individual family constellations? Take a couple that already has two youngsters, as of now. Suppose the wife submits to the inoculations for her next child and it's born with a size-mutation. How in the world will that child survive as a midget in a family of giants? There'll be untold damage to the personality—"

"We've heard all those arguments," Tom Lowery cut in. "The Naturalists have been handing out that line for years. What happens to the new generation of kids, how do we know they won't be mentally defective, how can they adjust, by what right does the government interfere with private lives, personal religious beliefs; all that sort of thing. For over ten years now the debate's been going on. And meanwhile, time is running out. Space is running out. Food is running out. It isn't a question of individual choice any longer—it's a question of group survival. I say the Courts are right. We have to go according to law. And back the law up with force of arms if necessary."

"We get the message," Januzki agreed. "But something tells me there'll be trouble. Most folks need a midget like they need a monkey on their backs."

"It's a gasser, pardners," said Nick Kendrick. "Naturalists don't dig this. They'll fight it all along the line. Everybody's gonna be all shook up."

"It is still a good idea," Lobo insisted. "This Dr. Leffingwell, he has made the tests. For years he has given injections and no harm has come. The children are healthy, they survive. They learn in special schools—"

"How do you know?" Bassett demanded. "Maybe it's all a lot of motivationalist propaganda."

"We have seen them on the telescreens, no?"

"They could be faking the whole thing."

"But Leffingwell, he has offered the shots to other governments beside our own. The whole world will adopt them—"

"What if some countries don't? What if our kids become midgets and the Asiatics refuse the inoculations?"

"They won't. They need room even more than we do."

"No sense arguing," Emil Grizek concluded. "It's the law. You know that. And if you don't like it, join the Naturalists." He chuckled. "But better hurry. Something tells me there won't be any Naturalists around after a couple of years. Now that there's a Leff Law, the government isn't likely to stand for too much criticism." He turned to Harry. "What do you think?" he asked.

Harry shrugged. "No comment," he said.

But the next day he went to Grizek and demanded his pay in full.

"Leaving?" Grizek muttered. "I don't understand. You've been with us almost five years. Where you going, what you intend to do? What's got into you all of a sudden?"

"Time for a change," Harry told him. "I've been saving my money."

"Don't I know it? Never touched a penny in all this time." Grizek ran a hand across his chin. "Say, if it's a raise you're looking for, I can—"

"No, thanks. It's not that. I've money enough."

"So you have. Around eighteen, twenty thousand, I reckon, what with the bonuses." Emil Grizek sighed. "Well, if you insist, that's the way it's got to be, I suppose. When you plan on taking off?"

"Just as soon as there's a 'copter available."

"Got one going up to Colorado Springs tomorrow morning for the mail. I can get you aboard, give you a check—"

"I'll want my money in cash."

"Well, now, that isn't so easy. Have to send up for a special draft. Take a week or so."

"I can wait."

"All right. And think it over. Maybe you'll decide to change your mind."

But Harry didn't change his mind. And ten days later he rode a 'copter into town, his money-belt strapped beneath his safety-belt.

From Colorado Springs he jetted to Kancity, and from Kancity to Memphisee. As long as he had money, nobody asked any questions. He holed up in cheap airtels and waited for developments.

It wasn't easy to accustom himself to urbanization again. He had been away from cities for over seven years now, and it might well have been seven centuries. The overpopulation problem was appalling. The outlawing of private automotive vehicles had helped, and the clearing of the airlanes served a purpose; the widespread increase in the use of atomic power cut the smog somewhat. But the synthetic food was frightful, the crowding intolerable, and the welter of rules and regulations attending the performance of even the simplest human activity past all his comprehension. Ration cards were in universal use for almost everything; fortunately for Harry, the black market accepted cash with no embarrassing inquiries. He found that he could survive.

But Harry's interest was not in survival; he was bent upon destruction. Surely the Naturalists would be organized and planning a way!

Back in '98, of course, they'd been merely an articulate minority without formal unity—an abstract, amorphous group akin to the "Liberals" of previous generations. A Naturalist could be a Catholic priest, a Unitarian layman, an atheist factory hand, a government employee, a housewife with strong prejudices against governmental controls, a wealthy man who deplored the dangers of growing industrialization, an Ag Culture worker who dreaded the dwindling of individual rights, an educator who feared widespread employment of social psychology, or almost anyone who opposed the concept of Mass Man, Mass-Motivated. Naturalists had never formed a single class, a single political party.

Surely, however, the enactment of the Leffingwell Law would have united them! Harry knew there was strong opposition, not only on the higher levels but amongst the general population. People would be afraid of the inoculations; theologians would condemn the process; economic interests, real-estate owners and transportation magnates and manufacturers would sense the threat here. They'd sponsor and they'd subsidize their spokesmen and the Naturalists would evolve into an efficient body of opposition.

So Harry hoped, and so he thought, until he came out into the cities; came out into the cities and realized that the very magnitude of Mass Man mitigated against any attempt to organize him, except as a creature who labored and consumed. Organization springs from discussion, and discussion from thought—but who can think in chaos, discuss in delirium, organize in a vacuum? And the common citizen, Harry realized, had seemingly lost the capacity for group action. He remembered his own existence years ago— either he was lost in a crowd or he was alone, at home. Firm friendships were rare, and family units survived on the flimsiest of foundations. It took too much time and effort just to follow the rules, follow the traffic, follow the incessant routines governing even the simplest life-pattern in the teeming cities. For leisure there was the telescreen and the yellowjackets, and serious problems could be referred to the psych in routine check-ups. Everybody seemed lost in the crowd these days.

Harry discovered that Dr. Manschoff had indeed lied to him; mental disorders were on the increase. He remembered an old, old book—one of the very first treatises on sociological psychology. *The Lonely Crowd*, wasn't it? Full of mumbo-jumbo about "inner-directed" and "outer-directed" personalities. Well, there was a grain of truth in it all. The crowd, and its individual members, lived in loneliness. And since you didn't know very many people well enough to talk to, intimately, you talked to yourself. Since you couldn't get away from physical contact with others whenever you ventured abroad, you stayed inside—except when you had to go to work, had to line up for food-rations or supplies, had to wait for hours for your check-ups on off-days. And staying inside meant being confined to the equivalent of an old-fashioned prison cell. If you weren't married, you lived in "solitary"; if you were married, you suffered the presence of fellow-inmates whose habits became intolerable, in time. So you watched the screen more and more, or you increased your quota of sedation, and when that didn't help you looked for a real escape. It was always available to you if you searched long enough; waiting at the tip of a knife, in the coil of a rope, the muzzle of a gun. You could find it at the very bottom of a bottle of pills or at the very bottom of the courtyard outside your window. Harry recalled looking for it there himself, so many years ago.

But now he was looking for something else. He was looking for others who shared not only his viewpoint but his purposefulness.

Where were the Naturalists?

Harry searched for several years.

The press?

But there were no Naturalists visible on the telescreens. The news and the newsmakers reflected a national philosophy adopted many generations ago by the Founding Fathers of mass-communication in their infinite wisdom—*"What's good for General Motors is good for the country."* And according to them, everything happening was good for the country; that was the cardinal precept in the science of autobuyology. There were no Arnold Ritchies left any more, and the printed newzine seemed to have vanished.

The clergy?

Individual churches with congregations in physical attendance, seemed difficult to find. Telepreachers still appeared regularly every Sunday, but their scripts—like everyone else's—had been processed in advance. Denominationalism and sectarianism had waned, too; all of these performers seemed very much alike, in that they were vigorous, forthright, inspiring champions of the *status quo.*

The scientists?

But the scientists were a part of the government, and the government was a one-party system, and the system supported the nation and the nation supported the scientists. Of course, there were still private laboratories subsidized for industrial purposes, but the men who worked in them seemed singularly disinterested in social problems. In a way, Harry could understand their position. It isn't likely that a dedicated scientist, a man whose specialized research has won him a Nobel Prize for creating a new detergent, will be worldly enough to face unpleasant realities beyond the walls of his antiseptic sanctum. After all, there was precedent for such isolationism—did the sainted Betty Crocker ever enlist in any crusades? As for physicians, psychiatrists and mass-psychologists, they were the very ones who formed the hard core of Leffingwell's support.

The educators, then?

Vocational Apt was a part of the government. And the poor pedagogues, who had spent generations hacking their way out of the blackboard jungles, were only too happy to welcome the notion of a coming millennium when their small charges would be still smaller. Even though formal schooling, for most youngsters, terminated at fourteen, there was still the problem of overcrowding. Telescreening and teletesting techniques were a help, but the problem was essentially a physical one. And Leffingwell was providing a physical solution. Besides, the educators had been themselves educated, through Vocational Apt. And while they, and the government, fervently upheld the principle of freedom of speech, they had to draw the line somewhere. As everyone knows, freedom of speech does not mean freedom to *criticize*.

Business men?

Perhaps there were some disgruntled souls in the commercial community, whose secret heroes were the oil tycoons of a bygone era or the old-time Stock Exchange clan united under the totems of the bull or the bear. But the day of the rugged individualist was long departed; only the flabby individualist remained. And he had the forms to fill out and the inspectors to contend with, and the rationing to worry about and the taxes to meet and the quotas to fulfill. But in the long run, he managed. The business man worked for the government, but the government also worked for him. His position was protected. And if the government said the Leff Shots would solve the overpopulation problem—*without* cutting down the number of consumers—well, was that really so bad? Why, in a generation or so there'd be even *more* customers! That meant increased property values, too.

It took Harry several years to realize he'd never find Naturalists organized for group action. The capacity for group action had vanished as the size of the group increased. All interests were interdependent; the old civic, fraternal, social and anti-social societies had no present purpose any more. And the once-familiar rallying-points—whether they represented idealistic humanitarianism or crass self-interest—had vanished in the crowd. Patriotism, racialism, unionism, had all been lost in a moiling megalopolitanism.

There were protests, of course. The mothers objected, some of them. Ag Culture, in particular, ran into difficulties with women who revived the quaint custom of "going on strike" against the Leff Law and refused to take their shots. But it was all on the individual level, and quickly coped with. Government medical authorities met the women at checkup time and demonstrated that the Leff Law had teeth in it. Teeth, and scalpels. The rebellious women were not subdued, slain, or segregated—they were merely sterilized. Perhaps more would have come of this if their men had backed them up; but the men, by and large, were realists. Having a kid was a headache these days. This new business of injections wasn't so bad, when you came right down to it. There'd still be youngsters around, and you'd get the same allotment for extra living space—only the way it worked out, there'd be more room and the kids would eat less. Pretty good deal. And it wasn't as if the young ones were harmed. Some of them seemed to be a lot smarter than ordinary—like on some of the big quizshows, youngsters of eight and nine were winning all those big prizes. Bright little ones. Of course, these must be the ones raised in the first special school the government had set up. They said old Leffingwell, the guy who invented the shots, was running it himself. Sort of experimenting to see how this new crop of kids would make out...

It was when Harry learned about the school that he knew what he must do.

And if nobody else would help him, he'd act on his own. There might not be any help from organized society, but he still had disorganized society to turn to.

He spent the next two years and the last of his money finding a way. The pattern of criminality had changed, too, and it was no easy matter to find the assistance he needed. About the only group crime still flourishing was hijacking; it took him a long while to locate a small under-cover outfit which operated around St. Louie and arrange to obtain a helicopter and pilot. Getting hold of the rifle was still more difficult, but he managed. And by the time everything was assembled, he'd found out what he needed to know about Dr. Leffingwell and his school.

As he'd suspected, the school was located in the old canyon, right in the same buildings which had once served as experimental units. How many youngsters were there, Harry didn't know. Maybe Manschoff was still on the staff, and maybe they'd brought in a whole new staff. These things didn't matter. What mattered was that Leffingwell was on the premises. And a man who knew his way about, a man who worked alone and to a single purpose, could reach him.

Thus it was that Harry Collins crouched behind the boulder that bright May morning and waited for Dr. Leffingwell to appear. The helicopter had dropped him at the upper end of the canyon the day before, giving him a chance to reconnoitre and familiarize himself with the terrain once again. He'd located Leffingwell's quarters, even seen the man through one of the lower windows. Harry had no trouble recognizing him; the face was only too familiar from a thousand 'casts viewed on a thousand screens. Inevitably, some time today, he'd emerge from the building. And when he did, Harry would be waiting.

He shifted behind the rocks and stretched his legs. Twelve years had passed, and now he'd come full circle. The whole business had started here, and here it must end. That was simple justice.

And it is justice, Harry told himself. *It's not revenge.* Because there'd be no point to revenge; that was only melodramatic nonsense. He was no Monte Cristo, come to wreak vengeance on his cruel oppressors. And he was no madman, no victim of a monomaniacal obsession. What he was doing was the result of lengthy and logical consideration.

If Harry Collins, longtime fugitive from a government treatment center, tried to take his story to the people, he'd be silenced without a hearing. But his story must be heard. There was only one way to arrest the attention of a nation— with the report of a rifle.

A bullet in Leffingwell's brain; that was the solution of the problem. Overnight the assassin would become a national figure. They'd undoubtedly try him and undoubtedly condemn him, but first he'd have his day in court. He'd get a chance to speak out. He'd give all the voiceless, unorganized victims of the Leff Law a reason for rebellion—and offer them an example. If Leffingwell had to die, it would be in a good cause. Moreover, he deserved to die. Hadn't he killed men, women, infants, without mercy?

But it's not revenge, Harry repeated. *And I know what I'm doing. Maybe I was disturbed before, but I'm sane now. Perfectly logical. Perfectly calm. Perfectly controlled.*

Yes, and now his sane, logical, calm, controlled eyes noted that the distant door was opening, and he sighted through the 'scope and brought his sane, logical, calm, controlled hand up along the barrel to the trigger. He could see the two men emerging, and the shorter, plumper of the two was Leffingwell. He squinted at the high forehead with its receding hairline; it was a perfect target. A little squeeze now and he knew what would happen. In his sane, logical, calm, controlled mind he could visualize the way the black hole would appear in the center of that forehead, while behind it would be the torn and dripping redness flecked with gray—

"What are you doing?"

Harry whirled, staring; staring down at the infant who stood smiling beside him. It *was* an infant, that was obvious enough, and implicit in the diminutive stature, the delicate limbs and the oversized head. But infants do not wear the clothing of pre-adolescent boys, they do not enunciate with clarity, they do not stare coolly and knowingly at their elders. They do not say, "Why do you want to harm Dr. Leffingwell?"

Harry gazed into the wide eyes. He couldn't speak.

"You're sick, aren't you?" the child persisted. "Let me call the doctor. He can help you."

Harry swung the rifle around. "I'll give you just ten seconds to clear out of here before I shoot."

The child shook his head. Then he took a step forward. "You wouldn't hurt me," he said, gravely. "You're just sick. That's why you talk this way."

Harry leveled the rifle. "I'm not sick," he muttered. "I know what I'm doing. And I know all about you, too. You're one of them, aren't you? One of the first of Leffingwell's brood of illegitimates."

The child took another step forward. "I'm not illegitimate," he said. "I know who I am. I've seen the records. My name is Harry Collins."

Somewhere the rifle exploded, the bullet hurtling harmlessly overhead. But Harry didn't hear it. All he could hear, exploding in his own brain as he went down into darkness, was the sane, logical, calm, controlled voice of his son.

CHAPTER SEVEN
Michael Cavendish—2027

Mike was just coming through the clump of trees when the boy began to wave at him. He shifted the clumsy old Jeffrey .475, cursing the weight as he quickened his pace. But there was no help for it, he had to carry the gun himself. None of the boys were big enough.

He wondered what it had been like in the old days, when you could get fullsized bearers. There used to be game all over the place, too, and a white hunter was king.

And what was there left now? Nothing but pygmies, all of them, scurrying around and beating the brush for dibatags and gerenuks. When he was still a boy, Mike had seen the last of the big antelopes go; the last of the wildebeestes and zebra, too. Then the carnivores followed—the lions and the leopards. *Simba* was dead, and just as well. These natives would never dare to come out of the villages if they knew any lions were left. Most of them had gone to Cape and the other cities anyway; handling cattle was too much of a chore, except on a government farm. Those cows looked like moving mountains alongside the average boy.

Of course there were still some of the older generation left; Kikiyu and even a few Watusi. But the free inoculations had begun many years ago, and the life-cycle moved at an accelerated pace here. Natives grew old and died at thirty; they matured at fifteen. Now, with the shortage of game, the elders perished still more swiftly and only the young remained outside the cities and the farm projects.

Mike smiled as he waited for the boy to come up to him. He wasn't smiling at the boy—he was smiling at himself, for being here. He ought to be in Cape, too, or Kenyarobi. Damned silly, this business of being a white hunter, when there was nothing left to hunt.

But somehow he'd stayed on, since Dad died. There were a few compensations. At least here in the forests a man could still move about a bit, taste privacy and solitude and the strange, exotic tropical fruit called loneliness. Even *that* was vanishing today.

It was compensation enough, perhaps, for lugging this damned Jeffrey. Mike tried to remember the last time he'd fired it at a living target. A year, two years? Yes, almost two. That gorilla up in Ruwenzori country. At least the boys swore it was *ingagi*. He hadn't hit it, anyway. Got away in the darkness. Probably he'd been shooting at a shadow. There were no more gorillas—maybe *they* had been taking the shots, too. Perhaps they'd all turned into rhesus monkeys.

Mike watched the boy run towards him. It was a good five hundred yards from the river bank, and the short brown legs couldn't move very swiftly. He wondered what it felt like to be small. One's sense of proportion must be different. And that, in turn, would affect one's sense of values. What values applied to the world about you when you were only three feet high?

Mike wouldn't know. He was a big man—almost five feet seven.

Sometimes Mike reflected on what things might be like if he'd been born, say, twenty years later. By that time almost everyone would be a product of Leff shots, and he'd be no exception. He might stay with people his own age in Kenyarobi without feeling self-conscious, clumsy, conspicuous. Pressed, he had to admit that was part of the reason he preferred to remain out here at Dad's old place now. He could tolerate the stares of the natives, but whenever he ventured into a city he felt awkward under the scrutiny of the young people. The way those teen-agers looked up at him made him feel a monster, rather.

Better to endure the monotony, the emptiness out here. Yes, and wait for a chance to hunt. Even though, nine times out of ten, it turned out to be a wild goose-chase. During the past year or so Mike had hunted nothing but legends and rumors, spent his time stalking shadows.

Then the villagers had come to him, three days ago, with their wild story. Even when he heard it, he realized it must be pure fable. And the more they insisted, the more they protested, the more he realized it simply couldn't be.

Still, he'd come. Anything to experience some action, anything to create the illusion of purpose, of—

"*Tembo!*" shrieked the boy, excited beyond all pretense of caution. "Up ahead, in river. You come quick, you see!"

No. It couldn't be. The government surveys were thorough. The last record of a specimen dated back over a half-dozen years ago. It was impossible that any survivors remained. And all during the safari these past days, not a sign or a print or a spoor.

"*Tembo!*" shrilled the boy. "Come quick!"

Mike cradled the gun and started forward. The other bearers shuffled behind him, unable to keep pace because of their short legs and—he suspected—unwilling to do so for fear of what might lie ahead.

Halfway towards the river bank, Mike halted. Now he could hear the rumbling, the unmistakable rumbling. And now he could smell the rank mustiness borne on the hot breeze. Well, at least he was down-wind.

The boy behind him trembled, eyes wide. He *had* seen something, all right. Maybe just a crocodile, though. Still some crocs around. And he doubted if a young native would know the difference.

Nevertheless, Mike felt a sudden surge of unfamiliar excitement, half expectancy and half fear. *Something* wallowed in the river; something that rumbled and exuded the stench of life.

Now they were approaching the trees bordering the bank. Mike checked his gun carefully. Then he advanced until his body was aligned with the trees. From here he could see and not be seen. He could peer down at the river—or the place where the river had been, during the rainy season long past. Now it was nothing but a mudwallow under the glaring sun; a huge mudwallow, pitted with deep, circular indentations and dotted with dung.

But in the middle of it stood *tembo*.

Tembo was a mountain, *tembo* was a black block of breathing basalt. *Tembo* roared and snorted and rolled red eyes.

Mike gasped.

He was a white hunter, but he'd never seen a bull elephant before. And this one stood eleven feet at the shoulders if it stood an inch; the biggest creature walking the face of the earth.

It had risen from the mud, abandoned its wallowing as its trunk curled about, sensitive to the unfamiliar scent of man. Its ears rose like the outspread wings of some gigantic jungle bat. Mike could see the flies buzzing around the ragged edges. He stared at the great tusks that were veined and yellowed and broken—once men had hunted elephants for ivory, he remembered.

But how could they? Even with guns, how had they dared to confront a moving mountain? Mike tried to swallow, but his throat was dry. The stock slipped through his clammy hands.

"Shoot!" implored the boy beside him. "You shoot, now!"

Mike gazed down. The elephant was aware of him. It turned deliberately, staring up the bank as it swayed on the four black pillars of its legs. Mike could see its eyes, set in a mass of grayish wrinkles. The eyes had recognized him.

They knew, he realized. The eyes knew all about him; who he was and what he was and what he had come here to do. The eyes had seen man before—perhaps long before Mike was born. They understood everything; the gun and the presence and the purpose.

"Shoot!" the boy cried, not bothering to hold his voice down any longer. For the elephant was moving slowly towards the side of the wallow, moving deliberately to firmer footing, and the boy was afraid. Mike was afraid, too, but he couldn't shoot.

"No," he murmured. "Let him go. I can't kill him."

"You must," the boy said. "You promise. Look—all the meat. Meat for two, three villages."

Mike shook his head. "I can't do it," he said. "That isn't meat. That's life. Bigger life than we are. Don't you understand? Oh, the bloody hell with it! Come on."

The boy wasn't listening to him. He was watching the elephant. And now he started to tremble.

For the elephant was moving up onto solid ground. It moved slowly, daintily, almost mincing as its legs sampled the surface of the shore. Then it looked up and this time there was no doubt as to the direction of its gaze—it stared intently at Mike and the boy on the bank. Its ears fanned, then flared. Suddenly the elephant raised its trunk and trumpeted fiercely.

And then, lowering the black battering-ram of its head, the beast came forward. A deceptively slow lope, a scarcely accelerated trot, and then all at once it was moving swiftly, swiftly and surely and inexorably towards them. The angle of the bank was not steep and the elephant's speed never slackened on the slope. Its right shoulder struck a sapling and the sapling splintered. It was crashing forward in full charge. Again it trumpeted, trunk extended like a flail of doom.

"Shoot!" screamed the boy.

Mike didn't want to shoot. He wanted to run. He wanted to flee the mountain, flee the incredible breathing bulk of this grotesque giant. But he was a white hunter, he was a man, and a man is not a beast; a man does not run away from life in any shape or size.

The trunk came up. Mike raised the gun. He heard the monster roar, far away, and then he heard another sound that must be the gun's discharge, and something hit him in the shoulder and knocked him down. Recoil? Yes, because the elephant wasn't there any more; he could hear the crashing and thrashing down below, over the rim of the river bank.

Mike stood up. He saw the boy running now, running back to the bearers huddled along the edge of the trail.

He rubbed his shoulder, picked up his gun, reloaded. The sounds from below had ceased. Slowly, Mike advanced to the lip of the bank and stared down.

The bull elephant had fallen and rolled into the wallow once more. It had taken a direct hit, just beneath the right ear, and even as Mike watched, its trunk writhed feebly like a dying serpent, then fell forward into the mud. The gigantic ears twitched, then flickered and flopped, and the huge body rolled and settled.

Suddenly Mike began to cry.

Damn it, he hadn't *wanted* to shoot. If the elephant hadn't charged like that—

But the elephant *had* to charge. Just as he *had* to shoot. That was the whole secret. The secret of life. And the secret of death, too.

Mike turned away, facing the east. Kenyarobi was east, and he'd be going there now. Nothing to hold him here in the forests any longer. He wouldn't even wait for the big feast. To hell with elephant-meat, anyway. His hunting days were over.

Mike walked slowly up the trail to the waiting boys.

And behind him, in the wallow, the flies settled down on the lifeless carcass of the last elephant in the world.

CHAPTER EIGHT
Harry Collins—2029

The guards at Stark Falls were under strict orders not to talk. Each prisoner here was exercised alone in a courtyard runway, and meals were served in the cells. The cells were comfortable enough, and while there were no telescreens, books were available—genuine, old-style books which must have been preserved from libraries dismantled fifty years ago or more. Harry Collins found no titles dated later than 1975. Every day or so an attendant wheeled around a cart piled high with the dusty volumes. Harry read to pass the time.

At first he kept anticipating his trial, but after a while he almost forgot about that possibility. And it was well over a year before he got a chance to tell his story to anyone.

When his opportunity came, his audience did not consist of judge or jury, doctor, lawyer or penologist. He spoke only to Richard Wade, a fellow-prisoner who had been thrust into the adjoining cell on the evening of October 11th, 2013.

Harry spoke haltingly at first, but as he progressed the words came more easily, and emotion lent its own eloquence. His unseen auditor on the other side of the wall did not interrupt or question him; it was enough, for Harry, that there *was* someone to listen at last.

"So it wasn't a bit like I'd expected," he concluded. "No trial, no publicity. I've never seen Leffingwell again, nor Manschoff. Nobody questioned me. By the time I recovered consciousness, I was here in prison. Buried alive."

Richard Wade spoke slowly, for the first time. "You're lucky. They might have shot you down on the spot."

"That's just what bothers me," Harry told him. "Why didn't they kill me? Why lock me up *incommunicado* this way? There aren't many prisons left these days, with food and space at such a premium."

"There are *no* prisons left at all—officially," Wade said. "Just as there are no longer any cemeteries. But important people are still given private burials and their remains secretly preserved. All a matter of influence."

"I've no influence. I'm not important. Wouldn't you think they'd consider it risky to keep me alive, under the circumstances? If there'd ever be an investigation—"

"Who would investigate? Not the government, surely."

"But suppose there's a political turnover. Suppose Congress want to make capital of the situation?"

"There is no Congress."

Harry gasped. "No Congress?"

"As of last month. It was dissolved. Henceforth we are governed by the Cabinet, with authority delegated to department heads."

"But that's preposterous! Nobody'd stand still for something like that!"

"They did stand still, most of them. After a year of careful preparation—of wholesale *exposes* of Congressional graft and corruption and inefficiency. Turned out that Congress was the villain all along; the Senators and Representatives had finagled tariff-barriers and restrictive trade-agreements which kept our food supply down. They were opposing international federation. In plain language, people were sold a bill of goods—get rid of Congress and you'll have more food. That did it."

"But you'd think the politicians themselves would realize they were cutting their own throats! The state legislatures and the governors—"

"Legislatures were dissolved by the same agreement," Wade went on. "There are no states any more; just governmental districts. Based upon sensible considerations of area and population. This isn't the old-time expanding economy based on obsolescence and conspicuous consumption. The primary problem at the moment is sheer survival. In a way, the move makes sense. Old-fashioned political machinery couldn't cope with the situation; there's no time for debate when instantaneous decisions are necessary to national welfare. You've heard how civil liberties were suspended during the old wars. Well, there's a war on right now; a war against hunger, a war against the forces of fecundity. In another dozen years or so, when the Leff shot generation is fullgrown and a lot of the elderly have died off, the tensions will ease. Meanwhile, quick action is necessary. Arbitrary action."

"But you're defending dictatorship!"

Richard Wade made a sound which is usually accompanied by a derisive shrug. "Am I? Well, I didn't when I was outside. And that's why I'm here now."

Harry Collins cleared his throat. "What did you do?"

"If you refer to my profession, I was a scripter. If you refer to my alleged criminal activity, I made the error of thinking the way you do, and the worse error of attempting to inject such attitudes in my scripts. Seems that when Congress was formally dissolved, there was some notion of preparing a timely show—a sort of historical review of the body, using old film clips. What my superiors had in mind was a comedy of errors; a cavalcade of mistakes and misdeeds showing just why we were better off without supporting a political sideshow. Well, I carried out the assignment and edited the films, but when I drafted a rough commentary, I made the mistake of taking both a pro and con slant. Nothing like that ever reached the telescreens, of course, but what I did was promptly noted. They came for me at once and hustled me off here. I didn't get a hearing or a trial, either."

"But why didn't they execute you? Or—" Harry hesitated—"is that what you expect?"

"Why didn't they execute *you*?" Wade shot back. He was silent for a moment before continuing. "No, I don't expect anything like that, now. They'd have done it on the spot if they intended to do so at all. No, I've got another idea about people like you and myself. And about some of the Congressmen and Senators who dropped out of sight, too. I think we're being stockpiled."

"Stockpiled?"

"It's all part of a plan. Give me a little time to think. We can talk again, later." Wade chuckled once more. "Looks as if there'll be ample opportunity in the future."

And there was. In the months ahead, Harry spoke frequently with his friend behind the wall. He never saw him—prisoners at Stark Falls were exercised separately, and there was no group assembly or recreation. Surprisingly adequate meals were served in surprisingly comfortable cells. In the matter of necessities, Harry had no complaints. And now that he had someone to talk to, the time seemed to go more swiftly.

He learned a great deal about Richard Wade during the next few years. Mostly, Wade liked to reminisce about the old days. He talked about working for the networks—the *commercial* networks, privately owned, which flourished before the government took over communications media in the '80s.

"That's where you got your start, eh?" Harry asked.

"Lord, no, boy! I'm a lot more ancient than you think. Why, I'm pushing sixty-five. Born in 1940. That's right, during World War II. I can almost remember the atomic bomb, and I sure as hell remember the sputniks. It was a crazy period, let me tell you. The pessimists worried about the Russians blowing us up, and the optimists were sure we had a glorious future in the conquest of space. Ever hear that old fable about the blind men examining an elephant? Well, that's the way most people were; each of them groping around and trying to determine the exact shape of things to come. A few of us even made a little money from it for a while, writing science fiction. That's how I got my start."

"You were a writer?"

"Sold my first story when I was eighteen or so. Kept on writing off and on for almost twenty years. Of course, Robertson's thermo-nuc formula came along in '75, and after that everything went to pot. It knocked out the chances of future war, but it also knocked out the interest in speculation or escape-fiction. So I moved over into television for a while, and stayed with it. But the old science fiction was fun while it lasted. Ever read any of it?"

"No," Harry admitted. "That was all before my time. Tell me, though—did any of it make sense? I mean, did some of those writers foresee what was really going to happen?"

"There were plenty of penny prophets and nickel Nostradamuses," Wade told him. "But as I said, most of them were assuming war with the Communists or a new era of space travel. Since Communism collapsed and space flight was just an expensive journey to a dead end and dead worlds, it follows that the majority of fictional futures were founded on fallacies. And all the rest of the extrapolations dealt with superficial social manifestations.

"For example, they wrote about civilizations dominated by advertising and mass-motivation techniques. It's true that during my childhood this seemed to be a logical trend—but once demand exceeded supply, the whole mechanism of *stimulating* demand, which was advertising's chief function, bogged down. And mass-motivation techniques, today, are dedicated almost entirely to maintaining minimum resistance to a system insuring our survival.

"Another popular idea was based on the notion of an expanding matriarchy—a gerontomatriarchy, rather, in which older women would take control. In an age when women outlived men by a number of years, this seemed possible. Now, of course, shortened working hours and medical advances have equalized the life-span. And since private property has become less and less of a factor in dominating our collective destinies, it hardly matters whether the male or the female has the upper hand.

"Then there was the common theory that technological advances would result in a push-button society, where automatons would do all the work. And so they might—if we had an unlimited supply of raw materials to produce robots, and unlimited power-sources to activate them. As we now realize, atomic power cannot be utilized on a minute scale.

"Last, but not least, there was the concept of a medically-orientated system, with particular emphasis on psychotherapy, neurosurgery, and parapsychology. The world was going to be run by telepaths, psychosis eliminated by brainwashing, intellect developed by hypnotic suggestion. It sounded great—but the conquest of physical disease has occupied the medical profession almost exclusively.

"No, what they all seemed to overlook, with only a few exceptions, was the population problem. You can't run a world through advertising when there are so many people that there aren't enough goods to go around anyway. You can't turn it over to big business when big government has virtually absorbed all of the commercial and industrial functions, just to cope with an ever-growing demand. A matriarchy loses its meaning when the individual family unit changes character, under the stress of an increasing population-pressure which eliminates the old-fashioned home, family circle, and social pattern. And the more we must conserve dwindling natural resources for people, the less we can expend on experimentation with robots and machinery. As for the psychologist-dominated society, there are just too many patients and not enough physicians. I don't have to remind you that the military caste lost its chance of control when war disappeared, and that religion is losing ground every day. Class-lines are vanishing, and racial distinctions will be going next. The old idea of a World Federation is becoming more and more practical. Once the political barriers are down, miscegenation will finish the job. But nobody seemed to foresee this particular future. They all made the mistake of worrying about the hydrogen-bomb instead of the sperm-bomb."

Harry nodded thoughtfully, although Wade couldn't see his response. "But isn't it true that there's a little bit of each of these concepts in our actual situation today?" he asked. "I mean, government and business *are* virtually one and the same, and they do use propaganda techniques to control all media. As for scientific research, look at how we've rebuilt our cities and developed synthetics for food and fuel and clothing and shelter. When it comes to medicine, there's Leffingwell and his inoculations. Isn't that all along the lines of your early science fiction?"

"Where's your Underground?" Richard Wade demanded.

"My *what?*"

"Your Underground," Wade repeated. "Hell, every science fiction yarn about a future society had its Underground! That was the whole gimmick in the plot. The hero was a conformist who tangled with the social order— come to think of it, that's what *you* did, years ago. Only instead of becoming an impotent victim of the system, he'd meet up with the Underground Movement. Not some sourball like your friend Ritchie, who tried to operate on his own hook, without real plans or system, but a complete *sub rosa* organization, bent on starting a revolution and taking over. There'd be wise old priests and wise old crooks and wise old officers and wise old officials, all playing a double game and planning a *coup*. Spies all over the place, get me? And in no time at all, our hero would be playing tag with the top figures in the government. That's how it worked out in all the stories.

"But what happens in real life? What happened to you, for example? You fell for a series of stupid tricks, stupidly perpetrated—because the people in power *are* people, and not the kind of synthetic super-intellects dreamed up by frustrated fiction-fabricators. You found out that the logical candidates to constitute an Underground were the Naturalists; again, they were just ordinary individuals with no genius for organization. As for coming in contact with key figures, you were actually on hand when Leffingwell completed his experiments. And you came back, years later, to hunt him down. Very much in the heroic tradition, I admit. But you never saw the man except through the telescopic sights of your rifle. That was the end of it. No modern-day Machiavelli has hauled you in to play cat-and-mouse games with you, and no futuristic Freud has bothered to wash your brain or soft-soap your subconscious. You just aren't that important, Collins."

"But they put me in a special prison. Why?"

"Who knows? They put me here, too."

"You said something once, about stockpiling us. What did you mean?"

"Well, it was just an old science fiction idea, I suppose. I'll tell you about it tomorrow, eh?"

And so the matter—and Harry Collins—rested for the night.

The next day Richard Wade was gone.

Harry called to him and there was no answer. And he cried out and he cursed and he paced his cell and he walked alone in the courtyard and he begged the impassive guards for information, and he sweated and he talked to himself and he counted the days and he lost count of the days.

Then, all at once, there was another prisoner in the adjacent cell, and his name was William Chang, and he was a biologist. He was reticent about the crime he had committed, but quite voluble about the crimes committed by others in the world outside. Much of what he said, about genes and chromosomes and recessive characteristics and mutation, seemed incomprehensible to Harry. But in their talks, one thing emerged clearly enough—Chang was concerned for the future of the race. "Leffingwell should have waited," he said. "It's the *second* generation that will be important. As I tried to tell my people—"

"Is that why you're here?"

Chang sighed. "I suppose so. They wouldn't listen, of course. Overpopulation has always been the curse of Asia, and this seemed to be such an obvious solution. But who knows? The time may come when they need men like myself."

"So you were stockpiled too."

"What's that?"

Harry told him about Richard Wade's remarks, and together they tried to puzzle out the theory behind them.

But not for long. Because once again Harry Collins awoke in the morning to find the adjoining cell empty, and once again he was alone for a long time.

At last a new neighbor came. His name was Lars Neilstrom. Neilstrom talked to him of ships and shoes and sealing-wax and the thousand and one things men will discuss in their loneliness and frustration, including—inevitably— their reasons for being here.

Neilstrom had been an instructor under Vocational Apt, and he was at a loss to explain his presence at Stark Falls. When Harry spoke of the stockpiling theory, his fellow- prisoner demurred. "It's more like Kafka than science fiction," he said. "But then, I don't suppose you've ever read any Kafka."

"Yes, I have," Harry told him. "Since I came here I've done nothing but read old books. Lately they've been giving me microscans. I've been studying up on biology and genetics; talking to Chang got me interested. In fact, I'm really going in for self-education. There's nothing else to do."

"Self-education! That's the only method left nowadays." Neilstrom sounded bitter. "I don't know what's going to become of our heritage of knowledge in the future. I'm not speaking of technological skill; so-called scientific information is carefully preserved. But the humanities are virtually lost. The concept of the well-rounded individual is forgotten. And when I think of the crisis to come—"

"What crisis?"

"A new generation is growing up. Ten or fifteen years from now we'll have succeeded in erasing political and racial and religious divisions. But there'll be a new and more dangerous differentiation; a *physical* one. What do you think will happen when half the world is around six feet tall and the other half under three?"

"I can't imagine."

"Well, I can. The trouble is, most people don't realize what the problem will be. Things have moved too swiftly. Why, there were more changes in the last hundred years than in the previous thousand! And the rate of acceleration increases. Up until now, we've been concerned about too rapid technological development. But what we have to worry about is social development."

"Most people have been conditioned to conform."

"Yes. That's our job in Vocational Apt. But the system only works when there's a single standard of conformity. In a few years there'll be a double one, based on size. What then?"

Harry wanted some time to consider the matter, but the question was never answered. Because Lars Neilstrom went away in the night, as had his predecessors before him. And in succeeding interludes, Harry came to know a half-dozen other transient occupants of the cell next to his. They came from all over, and they had many things to discuss, but always there was the problem of *why* they were there—and the memory of Richard Wade's premise concerning stockpiling.

There came a time when the memory of Richard Wade merged with the memory of Arnold Ritchie. The past was a dim montage of life at the agency and the treatment center and the ranch, a recollection of lying on the river bank with women in attitudes of opisthotonos or of lying against the boulders with a rifle.

Somewhere there was an image of a child's wide eyes and a voice saying, "My name is Harry Collins." But that seemed very far away. What was real was the cell and the years of talking and reading the microscans and trying to find a pattern.

Harry found himself describing it all to a newcomer who said his name was Austin—a soft-voiced man who became a resident of the next cell one day in 2029. And eventually he came to Wade's theory.

"Maybe there were a few wiser heads who foresaw a coming crisis," he concluded. "Maybe they anticipated a time when they might need a few nonconformists. People like ourselves who haven't been passive or persuaded. Maybe we're the government's insurance policy. If an emergency arises, we'll be freed."

"And then what would *you* do?" Austin asked, softly. "You're against the system, aren't you?"

"Yes. But I'm *for* survival." Harry Collins spoke slowly, thoughtfully. "You see, I've learned something through the years of study and contact here. Rebellion is not the answer."

"You hated Leffingwell."

"Yes, I did, until I realized that all this was inevitable. Leffingwell is not a villain and neither is any given individual, in or out of government. Our road to hell has been paved with only the very best of intentions. Killing the engineers and contractors will not get us off that road, and we're all on it together. We'll have to find a way of changing the direction of our journey. The young people will be too anxious to merely rush blindly ahead. Most of my generation will be sheeplike, moving as part of the herd, because of their conditioning. Only we old-time rebels will be capable of plotting a course. A course for all of us."

"What about your son?" Austin asked.

"I'm thinking of him," Harry Collins answered. "Of him, and of all the others. Maybe he does not need me. Maybe none of them need me. Maybe it's all an illusion. But if the time ever comes, I'll be ready. And meanwhile, I can hope."

"The time has come," Austin said, gently.

And then he was standing, miraculously enough, outside his cell and before the door to Harry's cell, and the door was opening. And once again Harry stared into the wide eyes he remembered so well—the same wide eyes, set in the face of a fullgrown man. A fullgrown man, three feet tall. He stood up, shakily, as the man held out his hand and said, "Hello, Father."

"But I don't understand—"

"I've waited a long time for this moment. I had to talk to you, find out how you really felt, so that I'd be sure. Now you're ready to join us."

"What's happening? What do you want with me?"

"We'll talk later." Harry's son smiled. "Right now, I'm taking you home."

CHAPTER NINE
Eric Donovan—2031

Eric was glad to get to the office and shut the door. Lately he'd had this feeling whenever he went out, this feeling that people were staring at him. It wasn't just his imagination: they did stare. Every younger person over a yard high got stared at nowadays, as if they were freaks. And it wasn't just the staring that got him down, either.

Sometimes they muttered and mumbled, and sometimes they called names. Eric didn't mind stuff like "dirty Naturalist." That he could understand—once upon a time, way back, everybody who was against the Leff Law was called a Naturalist. And before that it had still another meaning, or so he'd been told. Today, of course, it just meant anyone who was over five feet tall.

No, he could take the ordinary name-calling, all right. But sometimes they said other things. They used words nobody ever uses unless they really hate you, want to kill you. And that was at the bottom of it, Eric knew. They did hate him, they *did* want to kill him.

Was he a coward? Perhaps. But it wasn't just Eric's imagination. You never saw anything about such things on the telescreens, but Naturalists were being killed every day. The older people were still in the majority, but the youngsters were coming up fast. And there were so many *more* of them. Besides, they were more active, and this created the illusion that there were Yardsticks everywhere.

Eric sat down behind his desk, grinning. *Yardsticks.* When he was a kid it had been just the other way around. He and the rest of them who didn't get shots in those early days considered themselves to be the normal ones. And *they* did the name-calling. Names like "runt" and "half-pint" and "midgie." But the most common name was the one that stuck—Yardstick. That used to be the worst insult of all.

But now it wasn't an insult any more. Being taller was the insult. Being a dirty Naturalist or a son-of-a-Naturalist. Times certainly had changed.

Eric glanced at the communicator. Almost noon, and it had not flicked yet. Here he'd been beaming these big offers, you'd think he'd get some response to an expensive beaming program, but no. Maybe that was the trouble—nobody liked *big* things any more. Everything was small.

He shifted uneasily in his chair. That was one consolation, at least; he still had old-time furniture. Getting to be harder and harder to find stuff that fitted him these days. Seemed like most of the firms making furniture and bedding and household appliances were turning out the small stuff for the younger generation. Cheaper to make, less material, and more demand for it. Government allocated size priorities to the manufacturers.

It was even murder to ride public transportation because of the space-reductions. Eric drove his own jetter. Besides, that way was safer. Crowded into a liner with a gang of Yardsticks, with only a few other Naturalists around, there might be trouble.

Oh, it was getting to be a Yardstick world, and no mistake. Smaller furniture, smaller meals, smaller sizes in clothing, smaller buildings—

That reminded Eric of something and he frowned again. Dammit, why didn't the communicator flick? He should be getting some kind of inquiries. Hell, he was practically *giving* the space away!

But there was only silence, as there had been all during this past week. That's why he let Lorette go. Sweet girl, but there was no work for her here any more. No work, and no pay, either. Besides, the place spooked her. She'd been the one who suggested leaving, really.

"Eric, I'm sorry, but I just can't take this any more. All alone in this huge building—it's curling my toes!"

At first he tried to talk her out of it. "Don't be silly, luscious! There's Bernstein, down on ten, and Saltonstall above us, and Wallaby and Son on fourteen, I tell you, this place is coming back to life, I can feel it! I'll beam for tenants next week, you'll see—"

Actually he'd been talking against his own fear and Lorette must have known it. Anyway, she left. And now he was here alone.

Alone.

Eric didn't like the sound of that word. Or the absence of sound behind it. Three other tenants in a ninety-story building. Three other tenants in a place that had once held three thousand. Why, fifty years ago, when this place went up, you couldn't buy a vacancy. Where had the crowds gone to?

He knew the answer, of course. The Leff shots had created the new generation of Yardsticks, and they lived in their own world. Their shrunken, dehydrated world of dollhouses and miniatures. They'd deserted the old-fashioned skyscrapers and cut the big apartment buildings up into tiny cubicles; two could occupy the space formerly reserved for one.

That had been the purpose of the Leff shots in the first place—to put an end to overcrowding and conserve on resources. Well, it had worked out. Worked out too perfectly for people like Eric Donovan. Eric Donovan, rental agent for a building nobody wanted any more; a ninety-storey mausoleum. And nobody could collect rent from ghosts.

Ghosts.

Eric damned near jumped through the ceiling when the door opened and this man walked in. He was tall and towheaded. Eric stared; there was something vaguely familiar about his face. Something about those ears, that was it, those ears. No, it couldn't be, it wasn't possible—

Eric stood up and held out his hand. "I'm Donovan," he said.

The towheaded man smiled and nodded. "Yes, I know. Don't you remember me?"

"I thought I knew you from someplace. You wouldn't be—Sam Wolzek?"

The towheaded man's smile became a broad grin. "That's not what you were going to say, Eric. You were going to say 'Handle-head,' weren't you? Well, go on, say it. I don't mind. I've been called a lot worse things since we were kids together."

"I can't believe it," Eric murmured. "It's really you! Old Handle-head Wolzek! And after all these years, turning up to rent an office from me. Well, what do you know!"

"I didn't come here to rent an office."

"Oh? Then—"

"It was your name that brought me. I recognized it on the beamings."

"Then this is a social call, eh? Well, that's good. I don't get much company these days. Sit down, have a reef."

Wolzek sat down but refused the smoke. "I know quite a bit about your setup," he said. "You and your three tenants. It's tough, Eric."

"Oh, things could be worse." Eric forced a laugh. "It isn't as if my bucks depended on the number of tenants in the building. Government subsidizes this place. I'm sure of a job as long as I live."

"As long as you live." Wolzek stared at him in a way he didn't like. "And just how long do you figure that to be?"

"I'm only twenty-six," Eric answered. "According to statistics, that gives me maybe another sixty years."

"Statistics!" Wolzek said it like a dirty word. "Your life-expectancy isn't determined by statistics any more. I say you don't have sixty months left. Perhaps not even sixty days."

"What are you trying to hand me?"

"The truth. And don't go looking for a silver platter underneath it, either."

"But I mind my own business. I don't hurt anybody. Why should I be in any danger?"

"Why does a government subsidy support one rental manager to sit here in this building every day—but ten guards to patrol it every night?"

Eric opened his mouth wide before shaping it for speech. "Who told you that?"

"Like I said, I know the setup." Wolzek crossed his legs, but he didn't lean back. "And in case you haven't guessed it, this is a business call, not a social one."

Eric sighed. "Might have figured," he said. "You're a Naturalist, aren't you?"

"Of course I am. We all are."

"Not I."

"Oh yes—whether you like it or not, you're a Naturalist, too. As far as the Yardsticks are concerned, everyone over three feet high is a Naturalist. An enemy. Someone to be hated, and destroyed."

"Think I'd believe that? Sure, I know they don't like us, and why should they? We eat twice as much, take up twice the space, and I guess when we were kids we gave a lot of them a hard time. Besides, outside of a few exceptions like ourselves, all the younger generation are Yardsticks, with more coming every year. The older people hold the key positions and the power. Of course there's a lot of friction and resentment. But you know all that."

"Certainly." Wolzek nodded. "All that and more. Much more. I know that up until a few years ago, no Yardstick held any public office or government position. Now they're starting to move in, particularly in Europasia. But there's so many of them now—adults, in their early twenties—that the pressure is building up. They're impatient, getting out of hand. They won't wait until the old folks die off. They want control now. And if they ever manage to get it, we're finished for good."

"Impossible!" Eric said.

"Impossible?" Wolzek's voice was a mocking echo. "You sit here in this tomb and when somebody tells you that the world you know has died, you refuse to believe it. Even though every night, after you sneak home and huddle up inside your room trying not to be noticed, ten guards patrol this place with subatomics, so the Yardstick gangs won't break in and take over. So they won't do what they did down south—overrun the office buildings and the factories and break them up, cut them down to size for living quarters."

"But they were stopped," Eric objected. "I saw it on the telescreen, the security forces stopped them—"

"Crapola!" Wolzek pronounced the archaicism with studied care. "You saw films. Faked films. Have you ever traveled, Eric? Ever been down south and seen conditions there?"

"Nobody travels nowadays. You know that. Priorities."

"I travel, Eric. And I know. Security forces don't suppress anything in the south these days. Because they're made up of Yardsticks now; that's right, Yardsticks exclusively. And in a few years that's the way it will be up here. Did you ever hear about the Chicagee riots?"

"You mean last year, when the Yardsticks tried to take over the synthetic plants at the Stockyards?"

"Tried? They *succeeded*. The workers ousted management. Over fifty thousand were killed in the revolution—oh, don't look so shocked, that's the right word for it!—but the Yardsticks won out in the end."

"But the telescreen showed—"

"Damn the telescreen! I know because I happened to be there when it happened. And if *you* had been there, you and a few million other ostriches who sit with your heads buried in telescreens, maybe we could have stopped them."

"I don't believe it. I can't!"

"All right. Think back. That was last year. And since the first of this year, what's happened to the standard size meat-ration?"

"They cut it in half," Eric admitted. "But that's because of Ag shortages, according to the telescreen reports—" He stood up, gulping. "Look here, I'm not going to listen to any more of this kind of talk. By rights, I ought to turn your name in."

"Go ahead." Wolzek waved his hand. "It's happened before. I was reported when I blasted the Yardsticks who shot my father down when he tried to land his jet in a southern field. I was reported when they killed Annette."

"Annette?"

"You remember that name, don't you, Eric? Your first girl, wasn't she? Well, I'm the guy who married her. Yes, and I'm the guy who talked her into having a baby without the benefit of Leff shots. Sure, it's illegal, and only a few of us ever try it any more, but we both agreed that we wanted it that way. A real, life-sized, normal baby. Or abnormal, according to the Yardsticks and the stupid government.

"It was a dirty scum of a government doctor who let her die on the table when he discovered the child weighed seven pounds. That's when I really woke up, Eric. That's when I knew there was going to be only one decision to make in the future—kill or be killed."

"Annette. She died, you say?"

Wolzek moved over and put his hand on Eric's shoulder. "You never married, did you, Eric? I think I know why. It's because you felt the way I did about it. You wanted a regular kid, not a Yardstick. Only you didn't quite have the guts to try and beat the law. Well, you'll need guts now, because it's getting to the point where the law can't protect you any more. The government is made up of old men, and they're afraid to take action. In a few years they'll be pushed out of office all over the world. We'll have Yardstick government then, all the way, and Yardstick law. And that means they'll cut us down to size."

"But what can you—we—do about it?"

"Plenty. There's still a little time. If we Naturalists can only get together, stop being just a name and become an organized force, maybe the ending will be different. We've got to try, in any case."

"The Yardsticks are human beings, just like us," Eric said, slowly. "We can't just declare war on them, wipe them out. It's not their *fault* they were born that way."

Wolzek nodded. "I know. Nothing is anybody's fault, really. This whole business began in good faith. Leffingwell and some of the other geniuses saw a problem and offered what they sincerely believed was a solution."

"But it didn't work," Eric murmured.

"Wrong. It worked only too well. That's the trouble. Sure, we eliminated our difficulties on the physical level. In less than thirty years we've reached a point where there's no longer any danger of overcrowding or starvation. But the psychological factor is something we can't cope with. We thought we'd ended war and the possibilities of war a long time ago. But it isn't foreign enemies we must fear today. We've created a nation divided into Davids and Goliaths— and David and Goliath are always enemies."

"David killed Goliath," Eric said. "Does that mean we're going to die?"

"Only if we're as stupid as Goliath was. Only if we wear our telescreens like invincible armor and pay no attention to the slingshot in David's hands."

Eric lit a reef. "All right," he said. "You don't have to lecture. I'm willing to join. But I'm no Goliath, really. I never had a fight in my life. What could I do to help?"

"You're a rental agent. You have the keys to this building. The guards don't bother you by day, do they? You come and go as you please. That means you can get into the cellars. You can help us move the stuff down there. And we'll take care of the guards some night, after that."

"I don't understand."

The friendly pressure on Eric's shoulder became a fierce grip. "You don't have to understand. All you do is let us plant the stuff in the cellars and let us get rid of the guards afterwards in our own way. The Yardsticks will do the rest."

"You mean, take over the building when it's not protected?"

"Of course. They'll take it over completely, once they see there's no opposition. And they'll remodel it to suit themselves, and within a month there'll be ten thousand Yardsticks sitting in this place."

"The government will never stand still for that."

"Wake up! It's happening all over, all the time, and nothing is being done to prevent it. Security is too weak and officials are too timid to risk open warfare. So the Yardsticks win, and I'm going to see that they win this place."

"But how will that help us?"

"You don't see it yet, do you? And neither will the Yardsticks. Until, some fine day three or four months from now, we get around to what will be planted in the cellars. Somebody will throw a switch, miles away, and—boom!"

"Wolzek, you couldn't—"

"It's coming. Not only here, but in fifty other places. We've got to fight fire with fire, Eric. It's our only chance. Bring this thing out into the open. Make the government realize this is war. Civil war. That's the only way to force them to take real action. We can't do it any other way; it's illegal to organize politically, and petitions do no good. We can't get a hearing. Well, they'll have to listen to the explosions."

"I just don't know—"

"Maybe you're the one who should have married Annette after all." Wolzek's voice was cold. "Maybe you could have watched her, watched her scream and beg and die, and never wanted to move a muscle to do anything about it afterwards.

Maybe you're the model citizen, Eric; you and the thousands of others who are standing by and letting the Yardsticks chop us down, one by one. They say in Nature it's the survival of the fittest. Well, perhaps you're not fit to survive."

Eric wasn't listening. "She screamed," he said. "You heard her scream?"

Wolzek nodded. "I can still hear her. I'll always hear her."

"Yes." Eric blinked abruptly. "When do we start?"

Wolzek smiled at him. It was a pretty good smile for a man who can always hear screaming. "I knew I could count on you," he murmured. "Nothing like old friends."

"Funny, isn't it?" Eric tried to match his smile. "The way things work out. You and I being kids together. You marrying my girl. And then, us meeting up again this way."

"Yes," said Wolzek, and he wasn't smiling now. "I guess it's a small world."

CHAPTER TEN
Harry Collins—2032

Harry's son's house was on the outskirts of Washington, near what had once been called Gettysburg. Harry was surprised to find that it *was* a house, and a rather large one, despite the fact that almost all the furniture had been scaled down proportionately to fit the needs of a man three feet high.

But then, Harry was growing accustomed to surprises.

He found a room of his own, ready and waiting, on the second floor; here the furniture was of almost antique vintage, but adequate in size. And here, in an atmosphere of unaccustomed comfort, he could talk.

"So you're a physician, eh?" Harry gazed down into the diminutive face, striving to accept the fact that he was speaking to a mature adult. His own son—his and Sue's—a grown man and a doctor! It seemed incredible. But then, nothing was more incredible than the knowledge that he was actually here, in his child's home.

"We're all specialists in one field or another," his son explained. "Every one of us born and surviving during the early experimental period received our schooling under a plan Leffingwell set up. It was part of his conditional agreement that we become wards of the state. He knew the time might come when we'd be needed."

"But why wasn't all this done openly?"

"You know the answer to that. There was no way of educating us under the prevailing system, and there was always a danger we might be singled out as freaks who must be destroyed—particularly in those early years. So Leffingwell relied on secrecy, just as he did during his experimentation period. You know how *you* felt about that. You believed innocent people were being murdered. Would you have listened to his explanations, accepted the fact that his work was worth the cost of a few lives so that future billions of human beings might be saved? No, there was no time for explanation or indoctrination. Leffingwell chose concealment."

"Yes," Harry sighed. "I understand that better now, I think. But I couldn't see it then, when I tried to kill him." He flushed. "And I still can't quite comprehend why he spared me after that attempt."

"Because he wasn't the monster you thought him to be. When I pleaded with him—"

"*You* were the one!"

Harry's son turned away. "Yes. When I was told who you really were, I went to him. But I was only a child, remember that. And he didn't spare you out of sentimentality. He had a purpose."

"A purpose in sending me to prison, letting me rot all these years while—"

"While I grew up. I and the others like myself. And while the world outside changed." Harry's son smiled. "Your friend Richard Wade was right, you know. He guessed a great deal of the truth. Leffingwell and Manschoff and the rest of their associates deliberately set out to assemble a select group of nonconformists—men of specialized talents and outlooks. There were over three hundred of you at Stark Falls. Richard Wade knew why."

"And so he was dragged off and murdered."

"Murdered? No, Father, he's very much alive, I assure you. In fact, he'll be here tonight."

"But why was he taken away so abruptly, without any warning?"

"He was needed. There was a crisis, when Dr. Leffingwell died." Harry's son sighed. "You didn't know about that, did you? There's so much for you to learn. But I'll let him tell you himself, when you see him this evening."

Richard Wade told him. And so did William Chang and Lars Neilstrom and all the others. During the ensuing weeks, Harry saw each of them again. But Wade's explanation was sufficient.

"I was right," he said. "There was no Underground when we were at Stark Falls. What I didn't realize, though, was that there was an Overground."

"Overground?"

"You might call it that. Leffingwell and his staff formed the nucleus. They foresaw the social crisis which lay ahead, when the world became physically divided into the tall and the short, the young and the old. They knew there'd be a need of individuality then—and they *did* create a stockpile. A stockpile of the younger generation, specially educated; a stockpile of the older generation, carefully selected. We

105

conspicuous rebels were incarcerated and given an opportunity to think the problem through, with limited contact with one another's viewpoints."

"But why weren't we told the truth at the beginning, allowed to meet face-to-face and make some sensible plans for the future?"

Harry's son interrupted. "Because Dr. Leffingwell realized this would defeat the ultimate purpose. You'd have formed your own in-group, as prisoners, dedicated to your own welfare. There'd be emotional ties—"

"I still don't know what you're talking about. What are we supposed to prepare for now?"

Richard Wade shrugged. "Leffingwell had it all planned. He foresaw that when the first generation of Yardsticks— that's what they call themselves, you know—came of age, there'd be social unrest. The young people would want to take over, and the older generation would try to remain in positions of power. It was his belief that tensions could be alleviated only by proper leadership on both sides.

"He himself had an important voice in government circles. He set up an arrangement whereby a certain number of posts would be assigned to people of his choice, both young and old. Similarly, in the various professions, there'd be room for appointees he'd select. Given a year or two of training, Leffingwell felt that we'd be ready for these positions. Young men, like your son, would be placed in key spots where their influence would be helpful with the Yardsticks. Older men such as yourself would go into other assignments—in communications media, chiefly. The skillful use of group-psychological techniques could avert open clashes. He predicted a danger-period lasting about twenty years— roughly, from 2030 to 2050. Once we weathered that span, equilibrium would be regained, as a second and third generation came along and the elders became a small minority. If we did our work well and eliminated the sources of prejudice, friction and hostility, the transition could be made. The Overground in governmental circles would finance us. This was Leffingwell's plan, his dream."

"You speak in the past tense," Harry said.

"Yes." Wade's voice was harsh. "Because Leffingwell is dead, of cerebral hemorrhage. And his plan died with him. Oh, we still have some connections in government; enough to get men like yourself out of Stark Falls. But things have moved too swiftly. The Yardsticks are already on the march. The people in power—even those we relied upon—are getting frightened. They can't see that there's time left to train us to take over. And frankly, I'm afraid most of them have no inclination to give up their present power. They intend to use force."

"But you talk as though the Yardsticks were united."

"They are uniting, and swiftly. Remember the Naturalists?"

Harry nodded, slowly. "I was one, once. Or thought I was."

"You were a liberal. I'm talking about the *new* Naturalists. The ones bent on actual revolution."

"Revolution?"

"That's the word. And that's the situation. It's coming to a head, fast."

"And how will we prevent it?"

"I don't know." Harry's son stared up at him. "Most of us believe it's too late to prevent it. Our immediate problem will be survival. The Naturalists want control for themselves. The Yardsticks intend to destroy the power of the older generation. And we feel that if matters come to a head soon, the government itself may turn on us, too. They'll have to."

"In other words," said Harry, "we stand alone."

"Fall alone, more likely," Wade corrected.

"How many of us are there?"

"About six hundred," said Harry's son. "Located in private homes throughout this eastern area. If there's violence, we don't have a chance of controlling the situation."

"But we can survive. As I see it, that's our only salvation at the moment—to somehow survive the coming conflict. Then, perhaps, we can find a way to function as Leffingwell planned."

"We'll never survive here. They'll use every conceivable weapon."

"But since there's no open break with the government yet, we could still presumably arrange for transportation facilities."

"To where?"

"Some spot in which we could weather the storm. What about Leffingwell's old hideout?"

"The units are still standing." Harry's son nodded. "Yes, that's a possibility. But what about food?"

"Grizek."

"What?"

"Friend of mine," Harry told him. "Look, we're going to have to work fast. And yet we've got to do it in a way that won't attract any attention; not even from the government. I suggest we set up an organizing committee and make plans." He frowned. "How much time do you think we have—a year or so?"

"Six months," his son hazarded.

"Four, at most," Wade said. "Haven't you been getting the full reports on those riots? Pretty soon they'll declare a state of national emergency and then nobody will be going anywhere."

"All right." Harry Collins grinned. "We'll do it in four months."

Actually, as it worked out, they did it in just a day or so under three.

Five hundred and forty-two men moved by jetter to Colorado Springs; thence, by helicopter, to the canyon hideaway. They moved in small groups, a few each week. Harry himself had already established the liaison system, and he was based at Grizek's ranch. Grizek was dead, but Bassett and Tom Lowery remained and they cooperated. Food would be ready for the 'copters that came out of the canyon.

The canyon installation itself was deserted, and the only problem it presented was one of rehabilitation. The first contingent took over.

The jetters carried more than their human cargo; they were filled with equipment of all sorts—microscans and laboratory instruments and devices for communication. By the time the entire group was assembled, they had the necessary implementation for study and research. It was a well-conceived and well-executed operation.

To his surprise, Harry found himself acting as the leader of the expedition, and he continued in this capacity after they were established. The irony of the situation did not escape him; to all intents and purposes he was now ruling the very domain in which he had once languished as a prisoner.

But with Wade and Chang and the others, he set up a provisional system which worked out very well. And proved very helpful, once the news reached them that open revolt had begun in the world outside.

A battered 'copter landed one evening at dusk, and the wounded pilot poured out his message, then his life's blood.

Angelisco was gone. Washington was gone. The Naturalists had struck, using the old, outlawed weapons. And it was the same abroad, according to the few garbled reports thereafter obtainable only *via* ancient shortwave devices.

From then on, nobody left the canyon except on weekly 'copter-lifts to the ranch grazing lands for fresh supplies. Fortunately, that area was undisturbed, and so were its laconic occupants. They neither knew nor cared what went on in the world outside; what cities were reported destroyed, what forces triumphed or went down into defeat, what activity or radioactivity prevailed.

Life in the canyon flowed on, more peacefully than the river cleaving its center. There was much to do and much to learn. It was, actually, a monastic existence, compounded of frugality, abstinence, continence and devotion to scholarly pursuits. Within a year, gardens flourished; within two years herds grazed the grassy slopes; within three years cloth was being woven on looms in the ancient way and most of the homespun arts of an agrarian society had been revived. Men fell sick and men died, but the survivors lived in amity. Harry Collins celebrated his sixtieth birthday as the equivalent of a second-year student of medicine; his instructor being his own son. Everyone was studying some subject, acquiring some new skill. One-time rebellious natures and one-time biological oddities alike were united by the common bond of intellectual curiosity.

It was, however, no Utopia. Some of the younger men wanted women, and there were no women. Some were irked by confinement and wandered off; three of the fleet of eleven 'copters were stolen by groups of malcontents. From time to time there would be a serious quarrel. Six men were murdered. The population dwindled to four hundred and twenty.

But there was progress, in the main. Eventually Banning joined the group, from the ranch, and under his guidance the study-system was formalized. Attempts were made to project the future situation, to prepare for the day when it would be possible to venture safely into the outside world once again and utilize newly-won abilities.

Nobody could predict when that would be, nor what kind of world would await their coming. By the time the fifth year had passed, even shortwave reports had long since ceased. Rumors persisted that radioactive contamination was widespread, that the population had been virtually decimated, that the government had fallen, that the Naturalists had set up their own reign only to fall victim to internal strife.

"But one thing is certain," Harry Collins told his companions as they assembled in the usual monthly meeting on the grounds before the old headquarters building one afternoon in July. "The fighting will end soon. If we hear nothing more within the next few months, we'll send out observation parties. Once we determine the exact situation, we can plan accordingly. The world is going to need what we can give. It will use what we have learned. It will accept our aid. One of these days—"

And he went on to outline a carefully-calculated program of making contact with the powers that be, or might be. It sounded logical and even the chronic grumblers and habitual pessimists in the group were encouraged.

If at times they felt the situation fantastic and the hope forlorn, they were heartened now. Richard Wade summed it up succinctly afterwards, in a private conversation with Harry.

"It isn't going to be easy," he said. "In the old science fiction yarns I used to write, a group like this would have been able to prevent the revolution. At the very least, it would decide who won if fighting actually broke out. But in reality we were too late to forestall revolt, and we couldn't win the war no matter on whose side we fought. There's just one job we're equipped for—and that's to win the peace. I don't mean we'll step out of here and take over the world, either. We'll have to move slowly and cautiously, dispersing in little groups of five or six all over the country. And we'll have to sound out men in the communities we go to, find those who are willing to learn and willing to build. But we can be an influence, and an important one. We have the knowledge and the skill. We may not be chosen to lead, but we can *teach* the leaders. And that's important."

Harry smiled in agreement. They *did* have something to offer, and surely it would be recognized—even if the Naturalists had won, even if the entire country had sunk into semi-barbarism. No use anticipating such problems now. Wait until fall came; then they'd reconnoitre and find out. Wait until fall—

It was a wise decision, but one which ignored a single, important fact. The Naturalists didn't wait until fall to conduct their reconnaissance.

They came over the canyon that very night; a large group of them in a large jetter.

And they dropped a large bomb...

CHAPTER ELEVEN
Jesse Pringle—2039

They were after him. The whole world was in flames, and the buildings were falling, the mighty were fallen, the Day of Judgment was at hand.

He ran through the flames, blindly. Blind Samson. Eyeless in Gaza, treading at the mill. The mills of the gods grind slowly, but they grind exceedingly small.

Small. They were all small, but that didn't matter. They had the guns and they were hunting him down to his doom. Day of doom. Doomsday. The great red dragon with seven heads and ten horns was abroad in the land.

They had unleashed the dragon and his breath was a fire that seared, and his tail was a thunder that toppled towers.

The dragon was searching him out for his sins; he would be captured and set to labor in the mill.

But he would escape, he must escape! He was afraid of them, small as they were, and great oaks from little acorns grow, it's the little things that count, and he dare not go a-hunting for fear of little men.

Jesse crouched against the dock, watching the grain-elevators burn. The whole city was burning, Babylon the mighty, the whole world was burning in God's final wrath of judgment.

Nobody believed in God any more, nobody read the Bible, and that's why they didn't know these things. Jesse knew, because he was an old man and he remembered how it had been when he was a little boy. A little boy who learned of the Word of God and the Wrath of God.

He could see the reflection of the flames in the water, now, and the reflection was shimmery and broken because of the black clusters floating past. Large clusters and small clusters. There were bodies in the water, the bodies of the slain.

Thunder boomed from the city behind him. Explosions. That's how it had started, when the Naturalists began blowing up the buildings. And then the Yardsticks had come with their weapons, hunting down the Naturalists. Or had it been that way, really? It didn't matter, now. That was in another country and besides, the wench was dead.

The wench *is* dead. His wench, Jesse's wench. She wasn't so old. Only seventy-two. But they killed her, they blew off the top of her head and he could feel it when they did. It was as if something had happened in *his* head, and then he ran at them and screamed, and there was great slaughter amongst the heathen, the forces of unrighteousness.

And Jesse had fled, and smote evil in the name of the Lord, for he perceived now that the time was at hand.

How the mighty are fallen.

Jesse blinked at the water, wishing it would clear, wishing his thoughts would clear. Sometimes for a moment he could remember back to the way things *really* were. When it was still a real world, with real people in it. When he was just a little boy and everybody else was big.

Strange. Now he was an old man, a big old man, and almost everybody else was little.

He tried to think what it had been like, so long ago. It was too long. All he could remember about being small was that he had been afraid. Afraid of the bigger people.

And now he was big, and afraid of the smaller people.

Of course they weren't real. It was just part of the prophecy, they were the locusts sent to consume and destroy. He kept telling himself there was nothing to fear; the righteous need not fear when the day of judgment is at hand.

Only somewhere inside of him was this little boy, crying, "Mama, Mama, Mama!" And somewhere else was this old man, just staring down into the water and waiting for them to find him.

Another explosion sounded.

This one was closer. They must be bombing the entire city. Or else it was the dragon, lashing his tail.

Somebody ran past Jesse, carrying a torch. No, it wasn't a torch—his hair was on fire. He jumped into the water, screaming, "They're coming! They're coming!"

Jesse turned and blinked. They were coming, all right. He could see them pouring out of the alleyway like rats. Rats with gleaming eyes, gleaming claws.

Suddenly, his head cleared. He realized that he was going to die. He had, perhaps, one minute of life left. One minute out of eighty years. And he couldn't fool himself any longer. He was not delirious. Day of judgment—that was nonsense. And there was no dragon, and these were not rats. They were merely men. Puny little men who killed because they were afraid.

Jesse was a big man, but he was afraid, too. Six feet three inches tall he was, when he stood up straight as he did now, watching them come—but he knew fear.

And he resolved that he must not take that fear with him into death. He wanted to die with something better than that. Wasn't there something he could find and cling to, perhaps some memory—?

A minute is so short, and eighty years is so long. Jesse stood there, swaying, watching them draw nearer, watching them as they caught sight of him and raised their weapons.

He scanned rapidly into the past. Into the past, before the time the wench was dead, back to when you and I were young, Maggie, back still earlier, and earlier, seeking the high point, the high school, that was it, the high school, the highlight, the moment of triumph, the game with Lincoln. Yes, that was it. He hadn't been ashamed of being six feet three inches then, he'd been proud of it, proud as he raised his arms and—

Splashed down into the water as the bullets struck.

And that was the end of Jesse Pringle. Jesse Pringle, champion basketball center of the Class of '79...

CHAPTER TWELVE
Littlejohn—2065

The helicopter landed on the roof, and the attendants wheeled it over to one side. They propped the ladder up, and Littlejohn descended slowly, panting.

They had a coasterchair waiting and he sank into it, grateful for the rest. Hardy fellows, these attendants, but then they were almost three feet tall. More stamina, that was the secret. Common stock, of course, but they served a purpose. Somebody had to carry out orders.

When they wheeled the coasterchair into the elevator, Littlejohn descended. The elevator halted on the first floor and he breathed a sigh of relief. Great heights always made him faint and dizzy, and even a short helicopter trip took its toll—the mere thought of soaring two hundred feet above the ground was enough to paralyze him.

But this journey was vital. Thurmon was waiting for him.

Yes, Thurmon was waiting for him here in the council chamber. The coasterchair rolled forward into the room and again Littlejohn felt a twinge of apprehension. The room was vast—too big for comfort. It must be all of fifty feet long, and over ten feet in height. How could Thurmon stand it, working here?

But he had to endure it, Littlejohn reminded himself. He was head of the council.

Thurmon was lying on the couch when Littlejohn rolled in, but he sat up and smiled.

"I greet you," he said.

"I greet you," Littlejohn answered. "No, don't bother to stay seated. Surely we don't need to be ceremonious."

Thurmon pricked up his ears at the sound of the unfamiliar word. He wasn't the scholarly type, like Littlejohn. But he appreciated Littlejohn's learning and knew he was important to the council. They needed scholars these days, and antiquarians too. One has to look to the past when rebuilding a world.

"You sent for me?" Littlejohn asked. The question was purely rhetorical, but he wanted to break the silence. Thurmon looked troubled as he replied.

"Yes. It is a matter of confidence between us."

"So be it. You may speak in trust."

Thurmon eyed the door. "Come nearer," he said.

Littlejohn pressed a lever and rolled up to the couchside. Thurmon's eyes peered at him through the thick contact lenses. Littlejohn noted the deep wrinkles around his mouth, but without surprise. After all, Thurmon was an old man— he must be over thirty.

"I have been thinking," Thurmon said, abruptly. "We have failed."

"Failed?"

Thurmon nodded. "Need I explain? You have been close to the council for many years. You have seen what we've attempted, ever since the close of the Naturalist wars."

"A magnificent effort," Littlejohn answered politely. "In less than thirty years an entire new world has risen from the ruins of the old. Civilization has been restored, snatched from the very brink of a barbarism that threatened to engulf us."

"Nonsense," Thurmon murmured.

"What?"

"Sheer nonsense, Littlejohn. You're talking like a pedant."

"But I *am* a pedant." Littlejohn nodded. "And it's true. When the Naturalists were exterminated, this nation and other nations were literally destroyed. Worse than physical destruction was the threat of mental and moral collapse. But the Yardstick councils arose to take over. The concept of small government came into being and saved us. We began to rebuild on a sensible scale, with local, limited control. The little community arose—"

"Spare me the history lesson," said Thurmon, dryly. "We rebuilt, yes. We survived. In a sense, perhaps, we even made certain advances. There is no longer any economic rivalry, no social distinctions, no external pressure. I think I can safely assume that the danger of future warfare is forever banished. The balance of power is no longer a factor. The balance of

Nature has been partially restored. And only one problem remains to plague mankind."

"What is that?"

"We face extinction," Thurmon said.

"But that's not true," Littlejohn interrupted. "Look at history and—"

"Look at us." Thurmon sighed. "You needn't bother with history. The answer is written in our faces, in our own bodies. I've searched the past very little, compared to your scholarship, but enough to know that things were different in the old days. The Naturalists, whatever else they might have been, were strong men. They walked freely in the land, they lived lustily and long.

"Do you know what our average life-expectancy is today, Littlejohn? A shade under forty years. And that only if one is fortunate enough to lead a sheltered existence, as we do. In the mines, in the fields, in the radioactive areas, they die before the age of thirty."

Littlejohn leaned forward. "Schuyler touches on just that point in his *Psychology of Time*," he said, eagerly. "He posits the relationship between size and duration. Time is relative, you know. Our lives, short as they may be in terms of comparative chronology, nevertheless have a subjective span equal to that of the Naturalists in their heyday."

"Nonsense," Thurman said, again. "Did you think that is what concerns me—whether or not we feel that our lives are long or short?"

"What then?"

"I'm talking about the basic elements essential to survival. I'm talking about strength, stamina, endurance, the ability to function. That's what we're losing, along with the normal span of years. The world is soft and flabby. Yardstick children, they tell us, were healthy at first. But *their* children are weaker. And their grandchildren, weaker still. The effect of the wars, the ravages of radiation and malnutrition, have taken a terrible toll. The world is soft and flabby today. People can't walk any more, let alone run. We find it difficult to lift and bend and work—"

"But we won't have to worry about such matters for long," Littlejohn hazarded. "Think of what's being done in robotics. Those recent experiments seem to prove—"

"I know." Thurmon nodded. "We can create robots, no doubt. We have a limited amount of raw materials to allocate to the project, and if we can perfect automatons they'll function quite adequately. Virtually indestructible, too, I understand. I imagine they'll still be able to operate efficiently a hundred or more years from now—if only they learn to oil and repair one another. Because by that time, the human race will be gone."

"Come now, it isn't that serious—"

"Oh, but it is!" Thurmon raised himself again, with an effort. "Your study of history should have taught you one thing, if nothing else. The tempo is quickening. While it took mankind thousands of years to move from the bow and arrow to the rifle, it took only a few hundred to move from the rifle to the thermonuclear weapon. It took ages before men mastered flight, and then in two generations they developed satellites; in three, they reached the moon and Mars."

"But we're talking about *physical* development."

"I know. And physically, the human race altered just as drastically in an equally short span of time. As recently as the nineteenth century, the incidence of disease was a thousandfold greater than it is now. Life was short then. In the twentieth century disease lessened and life-expectancy doubled, in certain areas. Height and weight increased perceptibly with every passing decade. Then came Leffingwell and his injections. Height, weight, life-expectancy have fallen perceptibly every decade since then. The war merely hastened the process."

"You appear to have devoted a great deal of time to this question," Littlejohn observed.

"I have," answered the older man. "And it is not a question. It is a fact. The one fact that confronts us all. If we proceed along our present path, we face certain extinction in a very short time. The strain is weakening constantly, the vitality is draining away. We sought to defeat Nature—but the Naturalists were right, in their way."

"And the solution?"

Thurmon was silent for a long moment. Then, "I have none," he said.

"You have consulted the medical authorities?"

"Naturally. And experiments have been made. Physical conditioning, systems of exercise, experimentation in chemotherapy are still being undertaken. There's no lack of volunteers, but a great lack of results. No, the answer does not lie in that direction."

"But what else is there?"

"That is what I had hoped you might tell me," Thurmon said. "You are a scholar. You know the past. You speak often of the lessons of history—"

Littlejohn was nodding, but not in agreement. He was trying to comprehend. For suddenly the conviction came to him clearly; Thurmon was right. It was happening, had happened, right under their smug noses. The world was weakening. It was slowing down, and the race is only to the swift.

He cursed himself for his habit of thinking in platitudes and quotations, but long years of study had unfitted him for less prosaic phraseology. If he could only be practical.

Practical.

"Thurmon," he said. "There is a way. A way so obvious, we've all overlooked it—passed right over it."

"And that is—?"

"Stop the Leffingwell injections!"

"But—"

"I know what you'll say. There have been genetic mutations. Very true, but such mutations can't be universal. A certain percentage of offspring will be sound, capable of attaining full growth. And we don't have the population-problem to cope with any more. There's room for people again. So why not try it? Stop the injections and allow babies to be born as they were before." Littlejohn hesitated before adding a final word, but he knew he had to add it; he knew it now. "Normally," he said.

Thurmon nodded. "So that is your answer."

"Yes. I—I think it will work."

"So do the biologists," Thurmon told him. "A generation of normal infants, reared to maturity, would restore mankind to its former stature, in every sense of the word. And now, knowing the lessons of the past, we could prepare for the change to come. We could rebuild the world for them to live in, rebuild it psychically as well as physically. We'd plan to eliminate the rivalry between the large and the small, the strong and the weak. It wouldn't be difficult because there's plenty for all. There'd be no trouble as there was in the old days. We've learned to be psychologically flexible."

Littlejohn smiled. "Then that *is* the solution?" he asked.

"Yes. Eliminating the Leffingwell injections will give us a good proportion of normal children again. *But where do we find the normal women to bear them?*"

"Normal women?"

Thurmon sighed, then reached over and placed a scroll in the scanner. "I have already gone into that question with research technicians," he said. "And I have the figures here." He switched on the scanner and began to read.

"The average nubile female, aged thirteen to twenty-one, is two feet, ten inches high and weighs forty-eight pounds." Thurmon flicked the switch again and peered up. "I don't think I'll bother with pelvic measurements," he said. "You can already see that giving birth to a six or seven-pound infant is a physical impossibility under the circumstances. It cannot be done."

"But surely there must be *some* larger females! Perhaps a system of selective breeding, on a gradual basis—"

"You're talking in terms of generations. We haven't got that much time." Thurmon shook his head. "No, we're stopped right here. We can't get normal babies without normal women, and the only normal women are those who began life as normal babies."

"Which comes first?" Littlejohn murmured. "The chicken or the egg?"

"What's that?"

"Nothing. Just an old saying. From history."

Thurmon frowned. "Apparently, then, that's all you can offer in your professional capacity as an historian. Just some old sayings." He sighed. "Too bad you don't know some old prayers. Because we need them now."

He bowed his head, signifying the end of the interview.

Littlejohn rolled out of the room.

His 'copter took him back to his own dwelling, back across the rooftops of New Chicagee. Ordinarily, Littlejohn avoided looking down. He dreaded heights, and the immensity of the city itself was somehow appalling. But now he gazed upon the capital and center of civilization with a certain morbid affection.

New Chicagee had risen on the ashes of the old, after the war's end. Use of thermo-nucs had been limited, fortunately, so radioactivity did not linger, and the vast craters hollowed out by ordinary warheads had been partially filled by rubble and debris. Artificial fill had done the rest of the job, so that now New Chicagee was merely a flat prairie as it must have been hundreds of years ago—a flat prairie on which the city had been resurrected. There were almost fifty thousand people here in the capital; the largest congregation of population on the entire continent. They had built well and surely this time, built for the security and certainty of centuries to come.

Littlejohn sighed. It was hard to accept the fact that they had been wrong; that all this would end in nothingness. They had eliminated war, eliminated disease, eliminated famine, eliminated social inequality, injustice, disorders external and internal—and in so doing, they had eliminated themselves.

The sun was setting in the west, and long shadows crept over the city below. Yes, the sun was setting and the shadows were gathering, the night was coming to claim its own. Darkness was falling, eternal darkness.

It was quite dark by the time Littlejohn's 'copter landed on the rooftop of his own dwelling; so dark, in fact, that for a moment he didn't see the strange vehicle already standing there. Not until he had settled into his coasterchair did he notice the presence of the other 'copter, and then it was too late. Too late to do anything except sit and stare as the gigantic shadow loomed out of the night, silhouetted against the sky.

The shadow shambled forward, and Littlejohn gaped, gaped in terror at the titanic figure. He opened his mouth to speak, but words did not form; there were no words to form, for how does one address an apparition?

Instead, it was the apparition which spoke.

"I have been waiting for you," it said.

"Y-yes—"

"I want to talk to you." The voice was deep, menacing.

Littlejohn shifted in his coasterchair. There was nowhere to go, no escape. He gazed up at the shadow. Finally he summoned a response. "Shall we go inside?" he asked.

The figure shook its head. "Where? Down into that dollhouse of yours? It isn't big enough. I've already been there. What I have to say can be said right here."

"W-who are you?"

The figure stepped forward, so that its face was illuminated by the fluorescence streaming from the open door which led to the inclined chairway descending to Littlejohn's dwelling.

Littlejohn could see the face, now—the gigantic, wrinkled face, scarred and seared and seamed. It was a human face, but utterly alien to the humanity Littlejohn knew. Faces such as this one had disappeared from the earth a lifetime ago. At least, history had taught him that. History had not prepared him for the actual living presence of a—

"Naturalist!" Littlejohn gasped. "You're a Naturalist! Yes, that's what you are!"

The apparition scowled.

"I am not a Naturalist. I am a man."

"But you can't be! The war—"

"I am very old. I lived through your war. I have lived through your peace. Soon I shall die. But before I do, there is something else which must be done."

"You've come here to kill me?"

"Perhaps." The looming figure moved closer and stared down. "No, don't try to summon help. When your servants saw me, they fled. You're alone now, Littlejohn."

"You know my name."

"Yes, I know your name. I know the names of everyone on the council. Each of them has a visitor tonight."

"Then it is a plot, a conspiracy?"

"We have planned this very carefully, through the long years. It's all we lived for, those few of us who survived the war."

"But the council wasn't responsible for the war! Most of us weren't even alive, then. Believe me, we weren't to blame—"

"I know." The gigantic face creased in senile simulation of a smile. "Nobody was ever to blame for anything, nobody was ever responsible. That's what they always told me. I mustn't hate mankind for multiplying, even though population created pressure and pressure created panic that drove me mad. I mustn't blame Leffingwell for solving the overpopulation problem, even though he used me as a guinea-pig in his experiments. I mustn't blame the Yardsticks for penning me up in prison until revolution broke out, and I mustn't blame the Naturalists for bombing the place where I took refuge. So whose fault was it that I've gone through eighty years of assorted hell? Why did I, Harry Collins, get singled out for a lifetime of misery and misfortune?" The huge old man bent over Littlejohn's huddled form. "Maybe it was all a means to an end. A way of bringing me here, at this moment, to do what must be done."

"Don't harm me—you're not well, you're—"

"Crazy?" The old man shook his head. "No, I'm not crazy. Not now. But I *have* been, at times, during my life. Perhaps we all are, when we attempt to face up to the complications of an average existence, try to confront the problems which are too big for a single consciousness to cope with in a single life-span. I've been crazy in the city, and crazy in the isolation of a cell, and crazy in the welter of war. And perhaps the worst time of all was when I lost my son.

"Yes, I had a son, Littlejohn. He was one of the first, one of Leffingwell's original mutations, and I never knew him very well until the revolution came and we went away together. He was a doctor, my boy, and a good one. We spent almost five years together and I learned a lot from him. About medicine, but that wasn't important then. I'm thinking of what I learned about love. I'd always hated Yardsticks, but my son was one, and I came to love him. He had plans for rebuilding the world, he and I and the rest of us. We were going to wait until the revolution ended and then help restore sanity in civilization.

"But the Naturalists flew over and dropped their bomb, and my boy died. Over four hundred of our group died there in the canyon—four hundred who might have changed the fate of the world. Do you think I can forget that? Do you think I and the few others who survived have ever forgotten? Can you blame us if we did go crazy? If we hid away out there in the western wilderness, hid away from a world that had offered us nothing but death and destruction, and plotted to bring death and destruction to that world in return?

"Think about it for a moment, Littlejohn. We were old men, all of us, and the world had given us only its misery to bear during our lifetimes. The world we wanted to save was destroying itself; why should we be concerned with its fate or future?

"So we changed our plans, Littlejohn. Perhaps the shock had been too much. Instead of plotting to rebuild the world, we turned our thoughts to completing its destruction. Our tools and texts were gone, buried in the rubble with the bodies of fine young men. But we had our minds. Crazed minds, you'd call them—but aware of reality. The grim reality of the post-revolutionary years.

"We burrowed away in the desert. We schemed and we dreamed. From time to time we sent out spies. We knew what was going on. We knew the Naturalists were gone, that six-footers had vanished from a Yardstick world. We knew about the rehabilitation projects. We watched your people

126

gradually evolve new patterns of living and learning. Some of the former knowledge was rescued, but not all. Our little group had far more learning than you've ever dreamed of. Fifty of us, between ourselves, could have surpassed all your scientists in every field.

"But we watched, and we waited. And some of us died of privation and some of us died of old age. Until, at last, there were only a dozen of us to share the dream. The dream of destruction. And we knew that we must act swiftly, or not at all.

"So we came into the world, cautiously and carefully, moving unobtrusively and unobserved. We wanted to contemplate the corruption, seek out the weaknesses in your degenerate civilization. And we found them, immediately. Those weaknesses are everywhere apparent, for they are physical. You're one of a dying race, Littlejohn. Mankind's days are numbered. There's no need for grandiose schemes of reactivating warheads in buried missile-centers, of loosing thermo-nucs upon the world. Merely by killing off the central council here in New Chicagee, we can accomplish our objective. A dozen men die, and there's not enough initiative left to replace them. It's as simple as that. And as complicated."

Harry Collins nodded. "Yes, as complicated. Because the only weaknesses we've observed *are* physical ones. We've seen enough of the ways of this new civilization to realize that.

"All of the things I hated during my lifetime have disappeared now—the crowding, the competition, the sordid self-interest, the bigotry, intolerance, prejudice. The anti-social aspects of society are gone. There is only the human race, living much closer to the concept of Utopia than I ever dreamed possible. You and the other survivors have done well, Littlejohn."

"And yet you come to kill us."

"We came for that purpose. Because *we* still retained the flaws and failings of our former cultures. We looked for targets to blame, for villains to hate and destroy. Instead, we found this reality.

"No, I'm not crazy, Littlejohn. And I and my fellows aren't here to execute revenge. We have returned to the original plan; the plan Leffingwell had, and my son, and all the others who worked in their own way for their dream of a better world. We come now to help you. Help you before you die—before we die."

Littlejohn looked up and sighed. "Why couldn't this have happened before?" he murmured. "It's too late now."

"But it isn't too late. My friends are here. They are telling your fellow council-members the same thing right now. We may be old, but we can still impart what we have learned. There are any number of technological developments to be made. We can help you to increase your use of atomic power. There's soil reclamation and irrigation projects and biological techniques—"

"You said it yourself," Littlejohn whispered. "We're a dying race. That's the primary problem. And it's an insoluble one. Just this afternoon—" And he told him about the interview with Thurmon.

"Don't you understand?" Littlejohn concluded. "We have no solution for survival. We're paying the price now because for a while we wouldn't heed history. We tried to defeat Nature and in the end Nature has defeated us. Because we would not render unto Caesar the things which are—"

Harry Collins smiled. "That's it," he said.

"What?"

"Caesar. That's the answer. Your own medical men must have records. I know, because I learned medicine from my son. There used to be an operation, in the old days, called a caesarean section—used on normal women and on dwarfs and midgets too, in childbirth. If your problem is how to deliver normal children safely, the technique can be revived. Get hold of some of your people. Let's see what data you have on this. I'll be glad to furnish instruction—"

There was excitement after that. Too much excitement for Littlejohn. By the time the council had assembled in emergency session, by the time plans were formulated and he returned to his own dwelling in the helicopter, he was completely exhausted. Only the edge of elation sustained him; the realization that a solution had been found.

As he sank into slumber he knew that he would sleep the clock around.

And so would Harry Collins. The old man and his companions, now guests of the council, had been temporarily quartered in the council-chambers. It was the only structure large enough to house them and even so they had to sleep on the floor. But it was sufficient comfort for the moment.

It was many hours before Harry Collins awoke. His waking was automatic, for the tiny telescreen at the end of the council room glowed suddenly, and the traditional voice chirped forth to interrupt his slumber.

"Good morning," said the voice. "It's a beautiful day in New Chicagee!"

Harry stared at the screen and then he smiled.

"Yes," he murmured. "But tomorrow will be better."

THE END

If you've enjoyed this book, you will not want to miss these terrific titles...

ARMCHAIR SCI-FI, FANTASY, & HORROR DOUBLE NOVELS, $12.95 *each*

D-1   **THE GALAXY RAIDERS** by William P. McGivern
            SPACE STATION #1 by Frank Belknap Long

D-2   **THE PROGRAMMED PEOPLE** by Jack Sharkey
            SLAVES OF THE CRYSTAL BRAIN by William Carter Sawtelle

D-3   **YOU'RE ALL ALONE** by Fritz Leiber
            THE LIQUID MAN by Bernard C. Gilford

D-4   **CITADEL OF THE STAR LORDS** by Edmund Hamilton
            VOYAGE TO ETERNITY by Milton Lesser

D-5   **IRON MEN OF VENUS** by Don Wilcox
            THE MAN WITH ABSOLUTE MOTION by Noel Loomis

D-6   **WHO SOWS THE WIND...** by Rog Phillips
            THE PUZZLE PLANET by Robert A. W. Lowndes

D-7   **PLANET OF DREAD** by Murray Leinster
            TWICE UPON A TIME by Charles L. Fontenay

D-8   **THE TERROR OUT OF SPACE** by Dwight V. Swain
            QUEST OF THE GOLDEN APE by Ivar Jorgensen and Adam Chase

D-9   **SECRET OF MARRACOTT DEEP** by Henry Slesar
            PAWN OF THE BLACK FLEET by Mark Clifton.

D-10   **BEYOND THE RINGS OF SATURN** by Robert Moore Williams
            A MAN OBSESSED by Alan E. Nourse

ARMCHAIR SCIENCE FICTION CLASSICS, $12.95 each

C-1   **THE GREEN MAN**
            by Harold M. Sherman

C-2   **A TRACE OF MEMORY**
            By Keith Laumer

C-3   **INTO PLUTONIAN DEPTHS**
            by Stanton A. Coblentz

ARMCHAIR MASTERS OF SCIENCE FICTION SERIES, $16.95 each

M-1   **MASTERS OF SCIENCE FICTION, Vol. One**
            Bryce Walton: "Dark of the Moon" and other tales

M-2   **MASTERS OF SCIENCE FICTION, Vol. Two**
            Jerome Bixby: "One Way Street" and other tales

If you've enjoyed this book, you will not want to miss these terrific titles…

ARMCHAIR SCI-FI & HORROR DOUBLE NOVELS, $12.95 each

D-11   **PERIL OF THE STARMEN** by Kris Neville
THE STRANGE INVASION by Murray Leinster

D-12   **THE STAR LORD** by Boyd Ellanby
CAPTIVES OF THE FLAME by Samuel R. Delaney

D-13   **MEN OF THE MORNING STAR** by Edmund Hamilton
PLANET FOR PLUNDER by Hal Clement and Sam Merwin, Jr.

D-14   **ICE CITY OF THE GORGON** by Chester S. Geier and Richard Shaver
WHEN THE WORLD TOTTERED by Lester Del Rey

D-15   **WORLDS WITHOUT END** by Clifford D. Simak
THE LAVENDER VINE OF DEATH by Don Wilcox

D-16   **SHADOW ON THE MOON** by Joe Gibson
ARMAGEDDON EARTH by Geoff St. Reynard

D-17   **THE GIRL WHO LOVED DEATH** by Paul W. Fairman
SLAVE PLANET by Laurence M. Janifer

D-18   **SECOND CHANCE** by J. F. Bone
MISSION TO A DISTANT STAR by Frank Belknap Long

D-19   **THE SYNDIC** by C. M. Kornbluth
FLIGHT TO FOREVER by Poul Anderson

D-20   **SOMEWHERE I'LL FIND YOU** by Milton Lesser
THE TIME ARMADA by Fox B. Holden

ARMCHAIR SCIENCE FICTION CLASSICS, $12.95 each

C-4   **CORPUS EARTHLING**
by Louis Charbonneau

C-5   **THE TIME DISSOLVER**
by Jerry Sohl

C-6   **WEST OF THE SUN**
by Edgar Pangborn

ARMCHAIR SCIENCE FICTION & HORROR GEMS SERIES, $12.95 each

G-1   **SCIENCE FICTION GEMS, Vol. One**
Isaac Asimov and others

G-2   **HORROR GEMS, Vol. One**
Carl Jacobi and others

If you've enjoyed this book, you will not want to miss these terrific titles…

ARMCHAIR SCI-FI, FANTASY, & HORROR DOUBLE NOVELS, $12.95 each

D-21 **EMPIRE OF EVIL** by Robert Arnette
THE SIGN OF THE TIGER by Alan E. Nourse & J. A. Meyer

D-22 **OPERATION SQUARE PEG** by Frank Belknap Long
ENCHANTRESS OF VENUS by Leigh Brackett

D-23 **THE LIFE WATCH** by Lester Del Rey
CREATURES OF THE ABYSS by Murray Leinster

D-24 **LEGION OF LAZARUS** by Edmond Hamilton
STAR HUNTER by Andre Norton

D-25 **EMPIRE OF WOMEN** by John Fletcher
ONE OF OUR CITIES IS MISSING by Irving Cox

D-26 **THE WRONG SIDE OF PARADISE** by Raymond F. Jones
THE INVOLUNTARY IMMORTALS by Rog Phillips

D-27 **EARTH QUARTER** by Damon Knight
ENVOY TO NEW WORLDS by Keith Laumer

D-28 **SLAVES TO THE METAL HORDE** by Milton Lesser
HUNTERS OUT OF TIME by Joseph E. Kelleam

D-29 **RX JUPITER SAVE US** by Ward Moore
BEWARE THE USURPERS by Geoff St. Reynard

D-30 **SECRET OF THE SERPENT** by Don Wilcox
CRUSADE ACROSS THE VOID by Dwight V. Swain

ARMCHAIR SCIENCE FICTION CLASSICS, $12.95 each

C-7 **THE SHAVER MYSTERY, pt. 1**
by Richard S. Shaver

C-8 **THE SHAVER MYSTERY, pt. 2**
by Richard S. Shaver

C-9 **MURDER IN SPACE** by David V. Reed
by David V. Reed

ARMCHAIR MASTERS OF SCIENCE FICTION SERIES, $16.95 each

M-3 **MASTERS OF SCIENCE FICTION, Vol. Three**
Robert Sheckley, "The Perfect Woman" and other tales

M-4 **MASTERS OF SCIENCE FICTION, Vol. Four**
Mack Reynolds, "Stowaway" and other tales

A ROBOT COLONY RUN WILD!

To the naked eye they appeared to be nothing but a small group of robotic misfits. But the ruling robot, a surly pile of circuits and mechanisms named Bigboss, was sure that their tiny colony was the center of the universe. In fact, Bigboss was sure there was no other living creature that was superior to him in any way.

Yet a constant nagging deep in his robotic memory drums hinted of something different. It was a fleeting memory of the far-off world from which he came. A world where creatures lived that might actually challenge his rule. Little did he know that a spaceship filled with those creatures was hurtling towards him through the void. Living creatures of flesh and blood…

CAST OF CHARACTERS

DAVE STEWART
Something dreadful was lurking in this spaceman's mind, and the farther he traveled away from Earth, the worse it became.

CAROL CUMMINGS
She was as brilliant as she was beautiful—and her powers of direct radio empathy were crucial to her mission.

GABE RANDALL
He was one of the top men at the Bureau of Interstellar Exploration. What fearful secret did he carry with him into space?

CHANCELLOR VRAUSOT
This alien chancellor was a warrior at heart—all he wanted was the complete annihilation of the planet Earth.

ASSEMBLYMAN MITTICH
Unlike his war-mongering colleague, this alien politician sought peace for the galaxy. Could he prevent an all out war with Earth?

BIGBOSS
He thought he was the master of the universe, and at times he certainly appeared most formidable—but he was still just a robot.

NAT McALLISTER
His years in space should have made him a seasoned pro, but this veteran pilot was always likely to give his crew a bumpy ride.

REIGN OF THE TELEPUPPETS

By
DANIEL F. GALOUYE

ARMCHAIR FICTION
PO Box 4369, Medford, Oregon   97501-0168

*For more information about Armchair Books and products, visit our
website at…*

www.armchairfiction.com

Or email us at…

armchairfiction@yahoo.com

CHAPTER ONE

THE WAY this thing shapes up," Director Gabe Randall of the Bureau of Interstellar Exploration was saying in his usual manner of understatement, "it will be our most important trouble-shooting mission to date."

He stood crane-like, one leg hooked over a corner of the desk, as he whacked his thigh with an illuminated indicator rod. With purposeful eyes, he sized up the other three men in the briefing room. Lean and alert, he held himself straight against the encroachment of age that was evident in a fully white shock of hair and a brow furrowed with decades of executive responsibility.

"I suppose," he digressed, smiling, "that we'll have to get along without our Maid of the Megacycles."

Dave Stewart, Randall's assistant, glanced at the empty chair. "Carol said she'd be along shortly." Actually, she hadn't. But, if the situation were reversed, she'd cover for him.

"Woman's prerogative," the director observed, shrugging phlegmatically. "Gentlemen, I submit that the greatest deterrent to progress in BIE is the fact that direct radio empathy can be developed only in women—and young ones at that."

But Stewart recognized the imperceptible jocularity in the other's stare. It contrasted the sobriety with which he had said only a moment earlier that the nature of the mission required top personnel.

At half the director's age, Stewart had earned his recognition as logical successor to the seat of executive authority. And, in Carol Cummings, Randall had selected the most capable radio empathy specialist BIE had produced in years. The prettiest, too, he had added as an afterthought.

But there you could draw the line. Below was the *Photon II's* crew. At 44, Nat McAllister, pilot, was well past the age when he might look forward to a supervisory position, thanks to a rash of bad-judgment accidents and a general absence of ambition. And Ship Systems Officer Mortimer, ten years younger, seemed anchored to his niche by an equal measure of minimum ability—if not by the sheer weight of his two hundred and fifty pounds.

"Top" personnel for a "priority" job? Stewart shook his head dubiously.

RANDALL rapped the desk and the sharp sound snapped McAllister's chin from his chest, where it had gradually descended.

"Since it appears we'll continue to be disfavored by Miss Cummings' absence," the director resumed, "we'll proceed."

He touched a button and darkness filled the room. Another stud hurled into existence a ten-foot sphere of galactic luminosity, ablaze with motes of scattered brilliance.

Stewart located the co-ordinate axes and traced them to Sol. Nearby was Centauri, ringed with a halo to signify location of Headquarters, Bureau of Interstellar Exploration. Mortimer's corpulent face took on a Buddha-like appearance in the illumination from Alpha Hydrae, hovering near his left cheek.

"All right, Stewart," Randall gestured with his rod. "Suppose you identify that star immediately behind your shoulder for McAllister and Mortimer's benefit."

"Alpha Tauri."

"Right. Aldebaran—where you made a telepuppet drop on Four-B two years ago."

"Just before Harlston, and I pushed on out to explore beyond Aldebaran."

Randall directed his next words at the pilot and ship systems officer. "What Stewart did not know as he ranged outward was that the Aldebaran telepuppet team, for some reason, stopped transmitting—less than a year after the drop."

Stewart finger-combed a spray of blond hair off his forehead. In the pseudo galactic illumination his face, tanned from exposure to a score of suns radiating heavily in the ultraviolet range, appeared cinnamon in hue.

Randall glanced back at him. "Tell them what we're going to do on this mission."

"Unknot the puppet strings," he said laconically, becoming impatient with his dutiful recitation to enlighten the other two.

The director glanced off to his right, eyebrow raised to compound the eternal ridges of his forehead. "I see we've got our Maid of the Megacycles with us at last. Couldn't you tear yourself away from a Terracast, Miss Cummings? Or did you bring it along?"

Carol advanced through a patch of projected galactic nebulosity. Ebony hair sheening with the reflected glow, she smiled saucily and tapped her temple. "It so happens I *am* peeking in on a videocast," she bantered. "And I'm learning more about what's behind this briefing than if I'd been here all along."

Groping for her chair, she weaved between the steady, cold points of suspended light that represented Epsilon Scorpii and Eta Orphiuchi. "Don't look now, Chief," she added, winking, "but I'm afraid this newscast shows you've got a leak in your bureau."

Stewart caught her arm and guided her toward the chair. His hand held the coarse texture of fatigue coveralls that did little to obscure the shapeliness of her lithe, five-foot-four form.

She returned his greeting with a spirited, "Hi, glad to have you aboard. Not planning to lead us off on a two-year jaunt?"

Randall tapped the desk with his rod. "If Miss Cummings is willing to forego informalities, we can get along with our briefing."

McAllister tossed his head erect, but started nodding again almost immediately. Mortimer looked up tolerantly from contemplation on the orbiting of one of his stout thumbs around the other.

The director touched another button and the celestial sphere expanded to twice its diameter, encompassing another seventy light-years in all directions. "Again, directly behind you, Stewart, is—what?"

Enthusiastically, he sat erect. "The Hyades Cluster."

Randall laid down his rod. "Stewart, as you are aware, completed his expedition two weeks ago—in a ship stripped down for maximum range. Now he's going to tell us something about his experiences."

Mortimer, finally interested, glanced over at McAllister. The pilot, however, was dozing.

Stewart stared at the cluster of four stars huddled together in the still air of the briefing room. "We found the Hyades rich in Earth-type worlds. Seven—" He paused. Was it seven, or eight? "Eight of them are more like Terra than Terra itself. Four others are more suitable than anything we've run across in a century and a half of galactic exploration."

His eyes clung to the brilliant specs, set like jewels against a velvet background. They were jewels—cold and glittering and beckoning. And he could almost feel their attraction—like a magnet tugging on filings of hope and ambition. Yet, somehow he felt dejected, as though he was reluctant to reach out for them.

"You did *all* that in two years' time?" McAllister asked.

"Why yes, of course. I—" He could understand the other's skepticism, however. He *had* covered a lot of interstellar space.

"You all know what this development means," Randall said.

"That our expansion will be concentrated in a new direction!" Carol volunteered hopefully.

The chair creaked its complaint as Mortimer shifted his weight. "And the Aldebaran telepuppets?"

Randall gestured for emphasis. "That robot team is now of first-rate importance. We'll need a full analysis of Four-B in the shortest time possible. The Hyades are a hundred and fifty light-years away—too far for direct development. But a halfway base in the Aldebaran system will open them up to us immediately."

Carol found Stewart's arm. "This one is really worthwhile. Think you can get your puppets back on their strings?"

"I suppose so. There can't be too much wrong with them." But still his thoughts were on the Hyades. Somehow they left him with an emptiness, a bittersweet taste. Whereas he knew he should feel only enchantment and the satisfaction of accomplishment in his discovery.

"That all there is to this mission?" McAllister, fully awake now, asked disappointedly.

"I thought it was going to be a challenge," Mortimer complained.

Randall played the buttons on his desk as though they were a console keyboard. The celestial sphere deflated, then collapsed. Room lights blazed, harsh and intense. "Everything clear?" he asked.

Then he added, "We'll assemble at oh-eight-hundred Octoday at the *Photon II* dock. My gear is already packed."

Carol's eyes widened. "You're going too?"

"Yes, finally. About time I got out in the field and see how our new generation of...uh...specialists handles things."

Stewart only stared at the director. On the latter's desk were mountainous stacks of back work. Yet he was finding time to get away.

*   *   *

RATIONALIZATION circuits working sluggishly as he surveyed his realm, Bigboss dredged from the fragmented impressions on his memory drums his most fascinating, most disturbing subject for speculation:

In all Creation, there was nothing superior to Him. This material world that stretched out around Him, everything in the celestial reaches as far as infinity itself—all *His!* HQ had brought it into existence, although (confound those faulty drums!) He might not be able to recall the specific acts of Creation.

Yet He sensed, with the nagging certainty of conviction, that somewhere in His Universe, there was an insolent creature or creatures that would dare challenge His infinite supremacy.

Well (He generated power so fiercely that he had to shunt the excess to ground), let them! He could desire nothing more. And His only hope was that they would confront Him personally to express their insolence. *Then* there would be opportunity for an accounting!

Remembering his blaster, he swung around, aimed it at a boulder and, vengefully, fed it an enormous surge of power. Angry liquid light streaked out from the intensifier and crashed against the rock. The concussion sent him skittering back several meters.

Bigboss was by far the most magnificent member of the clan—if indeed, he should condescend to regard himself as belonging to the set at all. Fully twice the size of any of the others, he reared pompously erect on four stout appendages. Through its ports, his central section offered glowing evidence of the nuclear processes within. Majestic in stance, he swung a pair of formidable members—the auxiliary blaster and a massive, extensible vise.

Assuring himself that the insolent creatures were *not* spurious impressions on his drums, he blasted another boulder. *That* for the pretenders, should they ever, decide to contest His Reign!

Bigboss reacted abruptly to the realization that Minnie was watching him. No longer was his digital subsystem receiving her stream of telemetric signals. Relays clicked within his control section and video gain brought intensified visual awareness in all four quadrants. Immediately he spotted Minnie, immobile and ungainly as gyros balanced her elongated metal form on six jointed legs.

Her drill head, held high above the outcropping on which she had been working, glinted in the light of a shimmering, golden sun. Her single, wide-angle lens, set like a cyclopean eye in its chrome-plated forehead, was focused intently on him.

Interrupting his subliminal correlation of data from the other workers, he sent Minnie an indignant "back-to-work" impulse. Reluctantly, she sank her bit into the rock.

But she had ingested only a slotful of fragments when the ground bulged beside her. Displaced soil slid away and Screw Worm erupted, carrying in his thread pouches mineral specimens for her analyzers.

Bigboss generated more easily as he watched Worm at work. Not that the menial helper, who occupied the lowest rung on the ladder, was worthy of speculative attention. But a laboring borer meant Minnie was preoccupied with her limited supervisory function and couldn't be plotting to supplant him.

WORKING near Minnie, Seismo squatted at his sedentary task. Sensor rod sunk to bedrock, he was proudly purring an encoded disclosure of distant rumblings beneath the surface. Less than a hectometer away, Sky Watcher's tripodal locomotive system was bringing him carefully up a rise. Arriving, he assumed the location Sun Watcher had only recently abandoned. He adjusted himself on dead level, then thrust out a number of lensed tubes that locked on a referent star, three distant planets and a smaller satellite.

At that moment came an excited *eureka* impulse from Breather, posted outside a cave and briskly inflating and deflating the external pouches that bracketed his long, cylindrical form. The impulse proudly told of his detection of oxygen traces.

Nearby, Scraper diligently shoveled soil into his scoop in an endless search for microorganisms and DNA molecules. Grazer munched on a growth already identified as lichen. Peter the Meter sat on a knoll scanning the sky with his battery of inferometers, radiometers and bolometers.

Of the distant workers, Bigboss was most sensitively aware of the volant signals from Maggie. Kilometers away, she was covering the ground in great, leaping strides of abandon as she sought out and traced down each fascinating isomagnetic line of variation.

Work, work, work. Get the job done. Shake a leg. Shoulder (whatever that was) to the wheel. Dig in and pitch. But—for *what?*

What was responsible for the irresistible compulsion? Was it *his own* idea? But of course, it must be. For, how could there be any power capable of directing *Him?* Unless, perhaps, it might conceivably be the insolent creatures who lurked like vague shadows on the fringe of his almost obliterated memory. But, no!

He, Himself, was the Supreme Being of All Creation!

His master timer peaked in its four hundred-cycle sine wave, reminding him of the chore at hand. The sun had set and the huge, pink planet had already laid claim to the night sky. Just below it was the special grouping of stars that matched, point for point, the referent pattern on his orientation drum.

Programmed functions took over. Sensors hunted out the bright central star and aimed his parabolic antenna at the designated spot seven degrees southeastward. Then he loosed his transmission into subspace. Data stored over long hours of tedious sequencing surged from the tape, bringing a euphoria of relief.

Eventually telemetric transmission ended and Bigboss, as had become his custom, automatically turned his thoughts to the Totem.

All metal it was—sleek and sheening and shaped like a truncated cone as it lay powerless on the plain beyond the hill. How akin it was to him and the clan! Why, it even seemed he could almost *remember* having once been a part of the huge, polished thing. Perhaps it was the very vessel He had used on His Celestial Tour of Creation.

Yes, it was time for Pilgrimage to Totem. And a fitting reward it would be, as always, for successful transmission.

HE MUSTERED the volition required to break functional compulsion. Then he sent the "fall-in" impulse to his subjects. Eventually the line of march took shape, with

Bigboss leading his analyzers up the first hill and calling for the proper reverential attitude.

Behind him lumbered Minnie, her thick neck weighted by the bulky drill and swinging awkwardly with the sway of her six-legged stride. Seismo, encumbered with a faulty, dragging sensor rod, was having some difficulty maintaining a straight course.

Sky Watcher came along in lunging motions, a natural consequence of his tripodal system. Immediately to his rear, Sun Watcher, who held the fifth rung on the ladder, moved smoothly ahead with all his instruments retracted except the solar plasma detector.

Then there was a break in the line for Maggie, who could now be seen galloping along on an interceptive course. Peter the Meter, lurching from the imbalance of an extended boom-and-ball sensor, appeared somewhat like a many-spiked sphere on spindly legs.

Farther down the file, no deference was extended in the form of gaps for those missing workers who had yet to join the march.

Bringing up the rear were the diminutive Scraper and Grazer, resembling a pair of scurrying crabs, and Screw Worm, using his blade-edge jets to propel himself in a rolling, transverse motion.

Aware of commotion behind him, Bigboss continued unconcernedly up the rise. Sky Watcher, interpreting Seismo's faulty motions as an opportunity for his own forced ascendancy, had drawn back a photo-multiplier tube and sent it crashing into the other's rear plate.

The attack, though, was only self-thwarting, since it jarred a servo unit into retracting Seismo's dangling sensor rod. His locomotive integrity restored, he kicked out with a pedal pad and sent Sky Watcher flailing back into Sun Watcher. The latter rammed forward with his plasma detector's boom-and-ball shield, managing to knock Sky Watcher back into his proper position.

Finally fearful of damage to instruments, Bigboss gruffly radioed "cut-the-comedy" impulses, then trained his rearward lens on Minnie. She had inched furtively forward and was now menacing his upper section with her drill head.

He considered wielding his blaster but rejected that expedient as an excessive and unnecessary ostentation. Instead he countered by raising his extensible vise. The lesser show of strength sufficed to discourage Minnie's ambition, for the moment at least.

How foolish she was to imagine she could supplant Him as the Supreme Being!

Let her try.

Even if she succeeded, he would merely deny her a place at the trough next feeding period.

Then where would she get the vital charge for her batteries?

CHAPTER TWO

THE *Photon II* groaned, heaved and popped out of subspace for a fix before striking out on the last, short leg of its journey. As Stewart had feared, they were five light-years off course.

Ship Systems Officer Mortimer's thickly fleshed face struggled with an embarrassing smile. "Well, you can't hit 'em on the nose *every* time out," he rationalized, waddling back to the charts.

Stewart reflected that rare indeed were the occasions on which Mortimer came anywhere near the nasal target. Conceding the loss of nearly an entire day, he waited for Director Randall's permissive nod, then joined Mortimer in cutting the new navigation tapes.

It took two hours to process all data and feed them into the SCC-772. When the computer burped out the new heading, Stewart threaded the tape into the control programmer and decided to spend the uneventful period of subspace travel in his bunk.

Sleep came swiftly, but it was shallow and restless. More than once over the next several hours, as he plummeted down a chasm of nightmares, he regretted having left the control compartment.

First his dreams brought him back to the Hyadean Cluster, as they had on so many occasions during recent weeks. And for a while he drank in the blue-green beauty of the seven— or, was it eight?—worlds that seemed to beckon with all their irresistible allure.

They were incredibly splendorous, these planets that would soon embrace man and feed and clothe and shelter him. But, as he admired them in his dream, a sort of astronomical surrealism bunched them together—all in orbit around a central, massive sun—until it seemed they were occupying so compact an area that they must surely crumble under the weight of their mutual attraction.

And, as though upon his suggestion, crumble they did. Only, it was no pulverizing force that scattered them into fragmented rings, such as those around Sol's Saturn. Instead, each planet cracked like a hatching egg, its crust stripping away and exposing beneath a gruesome Harpy that was all razor-sharp talons and vicious beak and slime-filmed, ruffled feathers.

Stewart tried to scream himself awake but couldn't. He only flailed helplessly in the void while monstrous wings thrashed space into a frenzy, producing great currents that set the stars themselves to eddying and swirling.

They dived at him, but before their talons could sink into his flesh he awoke trembling and cold in his twisted, moist clothes.

For a long while he merely lay there trying to wash his mind of the horror. But the steady whine of the subspace drive reminded him that the *Photon* was streaking in the direction of the Hyades. That it would end its headlong plunge in the Aldebaran system, only halfway there, brought no relief from his baseless, unreasonable fear.

When he returned to the control compartment, the ship was back in normal space and within Aldebaran Four-B's gravitational field.

He joined Carol Cummings in the forward section, hooking his arm through a view-port strap and mooring himself against null gravity.

"You suppose we're home free?" she asked uncertainly.

Her normally effusive smile, he noticed, had moderated considerably. "If McAllister doesn't louse up his landing."

"I take it he's not very efficient."

"Pure and simple understatement. Last time out he missed an entire continent. It was a case for Search and Rescue."

Carol pressed forward and soft light from Aldebaran Four, off the port bow, warmed her sculpturesque features with primrose highlights. "I should imagine he would have been cashiered."

"But he wasn't. Instead he turns up on this *crucial* mission."

He busied himself with frequency adjustments on his portable transmitter. With it he would be able to tell, soon after landing, whether the Operations Coordinator could still be reached orally through its command discriminator circuit.

He flicked on the power switch, positioned the microphone comfortably against his larynx and sharply intoned a series of numerals. An oscilloscope faithfully traced the amplitude pattern, verifying effective transmission.

DOWN the companionway in the pilot's compartment, he could see McAllister anchored in his acceleration couch. He was drifting back and forth between padding and slack restraining straps, vicariously lost in the blood-and-guts action of a dramatape feeding into the view slot of his helmet.

Stewart read the label on the empty container— "The Kowalski Bros. in the Korean War."

"Always has his head buried in one of those escapist tapes, hasn't he?" Carol observed, still staring out the port.

"I don't think he ever grew up," Stewart agreed. But, again, even the Bureau seemed to contain its share of coasters who had never quite reached maturity, he remembered.

"Even in the Bureau," Carol observed thoughtfully, "you'll find coasters who've never reached maturity."

Intuitively, he tensed. Was it just coincidence that she had repeated, almost word for word, his own thoughts?

"I've never looked at any of those warfare tapes myself," she said. "But I've heard about them. Do you suppose armed conflict was really that horrible?"

"Pretty rough, according to the historians. It's not the sort of thing I'd like to be mixed up in."

"And McAllister?"

"Him? He's just building up a reservoir of false courage through his viewer." Yet, in fairness to the pilot, Stewart had to admit that he, himself, felt a deep and reasonable gratitude that wars were a thing of the historic past.

Carol sighed and glanced at him. "I'm certainly glad," she said, straight-faced, "that wars are a thing of the historic past."

He seized her arm. "Carol! Do you realize you're repeating *everything I'm thinking?* You've gone a step beyond radio empathy! You can pull in *thought* waves too!"

"No-o-o, you're joking!"

"No. Honest, I—" But his words were lost in her welling laughter.

He followed her amused stare to his portable voice transmitter and the mike that still clung to his throat. And instantly he realized that his sub-vocalizations, being picked up and broadcast, were to her like a window opening on his thought processes.

"Why, you—" Feigning indignation, he caught her around the waist and pulled her toward him. Weightless, she drifted forward and spread out conveniently across his knees.

But before he could bring a hand down resoundingly on the curvature of taut coveralls, Randall drifted in on the scene.

Still laughing, Carol straightened and announced, "Saved by the great, white-haired protector."

RANDALL grinned benignly, lighted his pipe and stared out the port. "Couldn't help hearing your conversation about the horror of warfare. I've seen all the documentary tapes. It was rough."

"Thank God it's a closed book," Carol said seriously.

"But, *is* it? There's still a large and articulate school that regards armed conflict as an instinctive human mechanism."

"We've had no war in two hundred years," Stewart said.

"Only because political subdivisions haven't had time for one. The instinct is blurred as a result of our expanding into a vacuum."

"I see." Carol's eyes strained with disillusionment. "And the question is—what happens when we run out of galaxy?"

"Fat chance." Stewart laughed. "We've got a few billion years to go before we find ourselves short on worlds."

Having apparently lost interest in the conversation, Randall was staring ahead at the onrushing satellite.

"That's one way of looking at it," Carol said pensively. "But there's also another possibility—resistance to the expansion."

"You kidding? In two centuries we haven't run into a single life form that's the intellectual equivalent of a Terran fiddler crab. What do you think, Chief?"

The director blew a stream of smoke at the swiftly expanding disc of Four-B. "I think our Maid of the Megacycles ought to start sniffing for that telepuppet team. I wouldn't want to rely on Mortimer's locating them with directional gear."

Carol faced the view port with her eyes closed for perhaps three minutes. Then she grinned. "I think I've got it! Not just a single, strong signal. Bundles of weak ones."

"It figures," Stewart verified. "The OC wouldn't be transmitting now. But the lesser puppets would be funneling the stuff into the CXB-1624. Can you identify any frequencies?"

She hesitated. "I'd say they're spaced out between fifteen hundred and two thousand kilocycles."

"You're a bit off. Should be sixteen to twenty-four hundred."

She opened her eyes, studied the rugged face of the satellite, then pointed. "There—near the end of that mountain range."

He handed her a mike and earphone set. "I'll tell McAllister you're ready to guide him in."

As Stewart had feared, McAllister's landing turned out to be a real corker. It even started with a three-gainer flip, rather than a simple end-about maneuver, when he first applied braking thrust.

*   *   *

"BIGBOSS responded automatically to the abruptly peaking sine wave that reminded him it was time for feeding. Summoning the clan with a brisk flow of "come-and-get it" signals on all command wavelengths, he strutted to the center of the clearing and prepared the trough. Squatting, he switched on all outlet circuits and directed bristling current into each jack.

The workers came from the cave, over the hills, out of the shadowy depths of fissures, from behind grotesque outcroppings. Illuminators piercing the twilight gloom, they extended retractable electrodes and converged on Bigboss.

One by one, plugs slipped into jacks and steadily increasing drain gave assurance of an orderly distribution of current.

Minnie was late arriving. She came along clumsily, massive drill head bobbing with her awkward stride. Had Bigboss' memory pack been serving him more efficiently at the time, he might have realized her gyros couldn't be overcorrecting that radically without triggering a "fix-me-I'm-broke" impulse.

But, as it was, she completed her apparently innocuous approach with impunity. Taking a last, measured step, she toppled over backwards on her posterior analyzing chamber. An ostensibly helpless victim of imbalance, her neck teetered skyward and her drill head hovered over Bigboss' upper section.

Then it crashed down, the drill bit shattering his port video pickup lens. Instantly he lost visual contact with one quadrant of his surroundings. He reacted at once, though, swiveling his upper section around ninety degrees and bringing Minnie back in sight through another lens. Guarding against repetition of the accident, he reached out and gripped her neck in his vise. He guided her plug into the proper jack, maintaining his purchase just to be sure.

Accident? he asked himself.

It was an unfamiliar concept, at best. Then he recalled that "mishap" was a notion not applicable to members of the clan. Perhaps other beings in other universes were given to blunder. In His World, though, He had arranged it that His intellects would be without error. Here the concept "intent" had no polar opposite.

Which meant that Minnie, not having reported malfunctioning gyros, had *planned* the destruction of one of his video sensors.

Vindictively, he started to turn upon her. But he realized he would be circumventing the primary compulsion—work, work, work. She was, after all, diligently discharging a worthwhile function in unraveling the secrets He had so cunningly hidden in His Creation.

FEEDING finally over, he signaled a general "back-to-work" order on all wavelengths and watched his subjects return to their chores, motions brisk with restored energy.

For many sine wave peaks thereafter, Bigboss fretted over the ramifications of having lost visual contact with a ninety-degree wedge of his environs. Had Minnie intended that effect? Did her rationalization pack have the capacity to reason out such a complex cause-and-effect relationship? Had she anticipated his resulting vulnerability?

Oh, he was compensating readily enough through self-reprogramming: stability for five sine wave saliences; activate upper section's horizontal servomechanism; circumrotate ninety degrees; stabilize; count five more waveform saliences;

reverse procedure. That way three video sensors did the job of four.

It gave him adequate coverage. But there were those times when the demands of function modification required the full output of his PM&R pack and his defensive scanning had to be sacrificed.

Such as now—when he was receiving Screw Worm's clear and frantic "save-me" signals.

Activating his directional gear, he lumbered over to the precise spot—a gentle rise of topsoil not far from where Minnie herself was chipping away at a boulder. Engaging his ventral illuminator-sensor, he located Worm's most recent drill hole. The borer's distress impulses were issuing with great amplitude from the opening. Bigboss unfolded his scoop and went to work.

It wasn't long before he had uncovered the borer's rearward axial protuberance. Extending his ventral vise, he gripped Worm securely, heaved to free him from the rock formation in which he had become wedged, and brought him back to the surface.

Released, the lesser worker scurried off to rejoin Minnie.

Bigboss realized only then that, during the entire rescue operation, he had neglected his defensive scanning procedure.

Restoring his upper section's quarterly rotational motion, he regarded Minnie warily. Was there any significance to the fact that she was facing him from the other side of the boulder, such that each time she elevated her head her field of vision swept over him?

Experimentally, he moved twenty meters to his right. Compensating, she skewed left, maintaining her visual advantage.

A calculated maneuver? Of course, it *had* to be. Perhaps her insolence should be dealt with summarily. But how could that be done without reducing the clan's over-all efficiency as a team dedicated to the compulsion of work, work, work?

AT THAT moment Peter the Meter, busy scanning the sky with his many of instruments, loosed a shrill *eureka* signal.

Bigboss thought for a moment that one of the latter's gamma ray spectrometers had been swamped. But, on monitoring Peter's telemetered stream, he discerned that the impulse was from an infrared photometer. A check of coordinates showed the source of disturbance to be skyward, with a dead zenith orientation.

He commandeered one of Sky Watcher's planetary telesensors and redirected it at the source of new emanation. Now there were additional data to throw light on the manifestation.

The disturbance was now in the visual range. It's classification—material. A rapidly shifting parallax suggested either constant location and swift expansion, or steady size and brisk approach.

Sky Watcher, on his own adaptive initiative, settled that uncertainty. His radar gear calculated a variable approach momentum averaging twelve hundred kilometers an hour and decreasing.

Peter also improvised on his function, bringing into play a photometer that instantly gauged the emissive intensity of the disturbance: comparable to the parameter for solar brilliance.

The object had shifted from zenith and was drifting over into the quadrant wherein the clan's Totem was located. Bigboss responded with some degree of concern to this development. Did it represent a threat to their revered symbol of metallic kinship?

Then he had the object in his own visual field. It was a great, blazing ball of brilliance that extended a flickering tongue downward. Atop the sphere of fiery energy sat a shining silver needle that resembled nothing as much as it did *the clan's own Totem!*

Evaluation circuits frozen in a confusion of indecision, he stood there fully unaware that he had discontinued his protective scanning and had not brought Minnie into one of his lines of sight for a number of sine wave epipeaks.

He was shocked back into action, however, when an equilibrium circuit tripped the alarm that his attitude was unstable and beyond compensation within the limits of gyroscopic control.

He pivoted sharply and planted two pedal discs down in the direction of fall. As he did so, his upper command section swung around, bringing a video lens to bear on Minnie. Refocusing, he saw she had crept up from his blind quadrant and had begun drilling into his power-plant section.

Fool. In her thirst for supremacy, didn't she realize she could touch off an explosion that would hurl them both halfway to the pink planet?

He pulled away from the grinding bite of her drill and brought his vise swinging forcibly upward. It slammed into her forward analyzing compartment and sent her reeling backward. Her equilibrium system over-extended, she toppled sideways and lay there kicking ineffectually.

By then, the great blazing light had disappeared beyond the hills at almost the exact site where the Totem was located.

He left Minnie to her struggles and went eagerly forward. Eventually, she would evaluate her position and hit upon the proper combination of responses to right herself.

Meanwhile the now surface-borne needle was a new environmental item that cried for analysis, with *eureka* signals already coming in from several workers. Maggie, for instance, was covering the ground in lurching strides, homing in one of the new lines of force the object had established.

Seismo had recorded and sent along exciting data on tremors that could be interpreted in terms of a number of closely-spaced, localized impacts. Even Minnie—despite her predicament and in response to the basic compulsion of her function—was using her high neutron tool. Evaluation circuits humming, she was sending a stream of signals that fairly screamed, "Pure metal!"

And Grazer, abandoning a patch of lichen, was scrambling up a hillside in the direction of the recently arrived object. His *eureka* was the most frenzied of all. Which was understandable, since he was sensing DNA molecules for the first time in his memory!

The best Bigboss could surmise, from a precursory correlation of data, was that Grazer had detected the molecules in a substance that wound helically around the great needlelike form.

Then his rationalization circuits labored under peak voltage as an obscure memory fragment thrust itself up from one of his drums.

Again, it was a vague bit concerning his suspicions on the existence of insolent creatures that might imagine themselves superior to Him—might even be presumptuous enough to give orders to the Supreme Being!

If such creatures were more than spurious impressions, he reasoned, then wasn't it likely that they, too, could move about in celestial vessels? Hadn't He all along feared that if they came to contest His Reign they would come from the sky?

Voltage regulators clicked frantically as he shunted aside raging current and averted damage to his rationalization pack. But he could hardly consider the beings without over-generating. They were *that* infuriating.

Had the contemptuous creatures come at last, as he had always supposed they would? Was his period of agonizing vigilance at an end? Could this be the final accounting he had anticipated so anxiously?

Enraged, he lumbered forward, his blaster extended rigidly before him, as though it was a lance.

CHAPTER THREE

STEWART dug out from under the miscellany of dislodged gear that had buried him in his acceleration couch.

"Good landing," he grumbled at McAllister, whose hands were still trembling at the controls, "—all six of them."

White-faced, Carol recovered her composure by releasing her hair from its free-fall net. "I wasn't sure," she whispered, "whether he was going to land or just play bounce."

Randall tested his legs. "Well, at least we *are* here."

He crossed over to the external view console and threw a switch. One of the screens flickered, then steadied with a wide-angle image of the sky, framed in the sweeping curvature of the horizon. Aldebaran, setting, was bisected by a serrate mountain range, while its fourth planet was rising in all its brilliant immensity.

More interested in their surface surroundings, however, Stewart brought another screen into play and aimed it at the ground. The lens swept across, then came back to focus on a silvery form that reared skyward beyond a nearby hill.

"At least McAllister put us down in the right place," he conceded. "There's the telepuppet barge—right where I left it."

He swung the lens on around and picked up movement on the ground almost in the shadow of the *Photon*.

"And there are our puppets!" Carol announced.

The Operations Coordinator, its laser intensifier evidently locked in the ready position, was leading a march toward the ship. Some of the team was not in evidence, as was to be expected after a year of managing on their own. But there was the Seismometer, the Astronomical Data Collector and the Solar Plasma Detector.

Trailing behind were the Atmosphere Analyzer and the Radiometer Complex. Stewart could make out even the lesser forms of the Microorganism Collector and Analyzer, the Flora C&A and the Subordinate Mineral Specimen Collector. In the distance, the Roving Magnetometer was homing in on the rest of the team.

He opened the locker and selected a hostile-atmosphere sheath. "This shouldn't take long. Just a matter of replacing the OC's malfunctioning unit. It's either a thermal increment problem or a component that's been ionized by particle radiation."

Reluctantly, Randall turned from the zenith screen. "How are you going to go about it?"

"Try a few oral commands on the OC." He slipped into the rubberized suit. "Trouble's probably in its CXB-1624 digital system."

"You picking up anything, Carol?" Randall asked.

She tilted her head alertly. "Just the subordinate stuff. I can't tell if the CXB's functioning 'til big boy starts transmitting to the relay station. However—"

She paused to stare curiously at Randall, who was still scrutinizing the sky. Stewart wondered momentarily whether the director might not be wrestling with a morbid fear of the astronomical distance separating him from home. It was possible, with Sol and Centauri far less prominent than Aldebaran's minor companions in the field of brilliant stars.

"However," Carol resumed, "I'll put on a sheath and go with you. Out there I might tap the pre-digital spill-off and find out whether it's correlating and sequencing properly."

"You'd better stay aboard for a while," Randall advised. "Those puppets haven't responded to human direction for over a year."

"You mean there might be danger?"

"Let's just say their behavior may not be entirely predictable." He gestured toward the screen. "Like now."

THE vanguard of robot explorers, led by the towering Operations Coordinator, had reached the ship. The Magnetometer began darting around one of the hydraulic fins, charting lines of isomagnetic intensity. The Mineral Analyzer had already sunk its drill into the broad, flat surface of the stabilizer. And the Flora Collector and Analyzer was being boosted by the OC to the lowest spiral of the ship's sub-space drive intensifier. Deposited upon the ceramics-insulated coil, the crab-like puppet was doing its best to flake off some of the outer substance for testing.

McAllister laughed. "Look at those mixed-up machines! They're trying to *analyze* the ship!"

"That's what I mean," Randall pointed out soberly. "One of their inhibitions is to ignore refined metal. That's how we keep their barges from being pecked to pieces."

"You don't think we can run into trouble out there, do you?" Mortimer asked, concerned.

Randall hesitated. "No, but we won't take any chances, although it's doubtful that loss of contact has obscured their *basic* inhibition."

"Of course it hasn't. Nothing like that's ever happened."

"In that case, you won't mind accompanying us outside."

Mortimer stabbed his chest with a pudgy thumb. *"Me?"*

"Right."

McAllister, Stewart noticed, was frowning in front of the screen as he watched the Flora C&A munching away at the subspace drive coil. "That thing can't do any damage, can it?"

"Not as long as the current's off," Stewart assured.

Mortimer paled as he lunged for the subspace drive switch.

But just then there was a thunderous concussion and the *Photon II* lurched and swayed on its hydraulic fins.

Randall shrugged. "Well, there goes our subspace drive."

"And our long-range transmitter too," Stewart added. "They both work off the same generator."

Outside, the puppets were withdrawing.

Mortimer, pulling up short of the switch, spread his arms apologetically. "I forgot to turn the circuit off."

Stewart grimaced. "Well, one thing's for sure: We're not going to finish up in a couple of hours and head for home."

Aiming the pickup lens more directly at the damaged area, Randall filled the screen with an image of shredded cable and shattered ceramics. "It'll take a week to repair that."

McAllister's face had whitened, causing the veins in his forehead to stand out under taut skin. "You mean we're stuck here?"

"As far as subspace is concerned. And I can't think of any lively spot we might want to visit in the Aldebaran system."

KEEPING a ridge of hills between themselves and the robots, Stewart trailed the telepuppet team towards their working area.

Randall stumbled and fell against him. Glancing back, he saw that the director had lost his footing because he was still staring at the sky. Within the helmet, his face appeared harsh and grim in the profuse coral planet-light.

Stewart shrugged, deciding to let the other wrestle in silence with his phobias, whatever they might be. As for himself, he had his own brand of jitters to worry about. And what made things worse was that he had no idea what was behind them.

Not that he hadn't been afraid before. One could hardly put in twelve years with the Bureau of Interstellar Exploration without getting his courage sullied somewhere along the way by a cliffhanger or two. But, in each of those cases, the menacing factor had been vivid, easily recognizable, something he could put his finger on.

The apprehension that lurked in the back of his mind now, however, was something he had never encountered before. Vague to the point of being mysterious, it seemed to be hardly more concrete than a fear of fear itself. But he felt that at any particular moment, if he found the right curtain to draw aside, he would expose a darkened recess filled with horror.

Was this dread something that was reaching up from the depths of his phantasmagoric nightmares? Was his subconscious, for some reason, handing up reservations on the acquisition of the Hyades as pearls on the string of galactic expansion? Intuition? Hunch?

Whatever it was, he didn't like it. And he cared for it even less now—as he trod the surface of this remote satellite and stared hypnotically ahead at the brilliant stars of the Hyades, well above the horizon. For how could he be certain *this* wasn't a nightmare and that in the next instant the stella ova wouldn't hatch and hurl their fierce Harpies at him?

"Why don't you try the big boy with a few commands?" Mortimer's voice rasped in his earphones. The ship systems officer, pulling up the rear, resembled an over-inflated balloon as he gestured at the line of telepuppets through a breach in the ridge.

Satisfied with the concealment their present position offered, Stewart flipped on the command transmitter and intoned, "Supervisor to OC. Stabilize and remain where you are."

The master robot didn't even break stride.

He tried the order again, then repeated it several times as he tuned slightly up and down the band.

"It's no use," he said finally. "Either the thing's slipped frequency, or it's not receiving at all."

"Carol will spot any new wave length," Randall assured.

"What we ought to do," Mortimer proposed impatiently, "is show that thing who's boss."

Then Stewart caught the motion in the corner of his eye as the ship systems officer struck out for the marching file of puppets.

He intercepted the line near the tail end and tried to force his way in between the Solar Plasma Detector and the Magnetometer so he could close in on the OC. But the SPD kicked out with a stiff pedal pad and sent him sprawling in the path of the Magnetometer, which simply strode over him.

The Atmosphere Analyzer nudged him aside with an inflated air pouch and, in its turn, the Radiometer Complex compounded the indignity by planting a motor appendage in his abdomen. Mortimer rose screaming, circled wide around the Micro-organism C&A and the Subordinate Mineral Specimen Collector and raced for the ship.

"This," said Stewart, "may not be as simple as we thought. Evidently some basic inhibitions have faded."

"We can't risk getting in range of one of those larger puppets, especially the OC," Randall agreed.

Abruptly the master robot stabilized, swung sharply to face the horizon and adjusted its parabolic antenna.

"Look!" Stewart pointed. "The thing's transmitting! But it's not properly oriented! *It's beaming in the wrong direction!*"

"Where's it transmitting to?" Randall asked anxiously.

"Can't tell without point-to-point astrographs. Anyway, what difference does it make? It's only a random misorientation."

On the way back to the *Photon II*, Stewart lost himself in confusion. Random misorientation? Of course. What else? But why should he even consider the alternate possibility—that the misorientation was *not* random, as suggested by the director's question?

* * *

BIG BOSS completed transmission and burst into an instant fury of thwarted purpose. He leveled his blaster and annihilated the ridge behind which the defiant mobiles had recently hidden.

He swiveled his central section, redirecting the blaster at a boulder that lay between him and the needle and destroying it in a fiery eruption of light and heat and pulverizing forces.

Fuming, he paced forward, stopped and paced back again. He had *seen* the audacious creatures that were bold enough to invade His Realm! But He had been able to do nothing about them. For at that moment the irresistible compulsion of function had taken over and He could only orient and transmit all the data from his master tape.

Surlily, he bled off excessive current in his reaction circuits and watched his workers going dutifully about their business. Inactivity was frustrating, of course, but it was not entirely unwelcome. For there was much now that demanded evaluation, even though his urge to pursue the contemptuous mobiles and blast them from their needle was almost overpowering.

For one thing, there was the needle itself. Had He made it? (Oh, why couldn't he *remember* these things?) Of course, He must have, although he couldn't recall the specific act of

Creation. And he must have produced the arrogant mobiles too, even though they would probably claim *they* had created *Him*.

But the needle itself was *metal!* Even a precursory analysis with Minnie's high neutron flux tools had established this. It was *so* much like the clan's Totem it must be Totemic.

The evidence was undeniable. Every member of the clan was metal. The clan's Totem was metal. Therefore the new thing from the sky was to be revered as the traditional Totem was.

Hence he had been justified, he assured himself, in issuing the "cease-and-desist" order that had brought an end to destructive analysis of the needle.

But, still, it was providing sanctuary for the detestable little mobiles, which comprised a frustration that was almost unbearable. A venerable Totem offering protection to the arrogant non-Totemic creatures that had to be destroyed so His Universe would be cleansed of their blasphemous impudence!

The demands of logical deduction fully served, he published on each wavelength an order that amounted to: "Vigilance is to be maintained against the non-Totemic mobiles. Report instantly on their reappearance."

That taken care of, he reduced current in his rationalization pack. But the pleasant calm of abstraction did not last long. Peter the Meter began flooding his allocated frequency with *eureka* signals from an infrared photometer. And once again the source of disturbance was at a remote distance in the sky.

Oh Bigboss, he invoked Himself. Not *another* Totemic-non-Totemic complication!

As before, Sky Watcher accepted the reported coordinates and trained a visual telesensor on the indicated position. But nothing was there. His doppler radar gear, however, did manage to pick up a blip at many hundred kilometers' distance just as it vanished.

Only a meteor, Bigboss decided, relieved. He let the evaluation stand, even though Peter the Meter had detected no ionized trail that would have verified that type of disturbance.

And Bigboss generated a good deal more easily, satisfied that the new manifestation had not, after all, been *another* needle.

His peace of rationalization pack was fleeting indeed, however. For in the next moment it required the full versatility of all his servomechanisms to maintain balance against a sudden upheaval of the ground beneath one of his appendages.

Tottering precariously, he engaged his underslung illuminator and video sensor. Screw Worm, having evidently bored a great distance, was emerging at the spot where his foot pad had been planted.

Fifty meters off, Minnie was expectantly rigid, her lens aimed in his direction. She was poised for a running start toward him should the opportunity present itself.

Screw Worm finally surfaced. Angrily, Bigboss kicked him back toward Minnie, who returned—disappointed, it seemed—to her work.

* * *

THE HUGE Tzarean ship, bristling with the most formidable weapons its makers had devised in millennia, recovered from subspace emergency, adjusted its concealment shield and slipped into orbit.

Assemblyman Mittich, second in command, used a stout tail to brace himself against shifting inertia and watched

REIGN OF THE TELEPUPPETS

Vrausot, Chancellor of the Tzarean Shoal, hiss his nagging instructions.

"The data, Kavula!" he demanded. "Punch out the data!"

Cowering before the impatience of the Tzarean Worlds highest authority, the pilot beat upon the control computer with a taloned fist. "It will be feeding out soon—I hope."

Mittich pressed forward into the anxiety that filled the compartment with hydrostatic-like intensity. It was well past time for his isotonic saline soaking and already the coarse drying process was chafing his chitinous skin. He was even sensitively aware of each scale as it grated against the one beneath it.

But he couldn't withdraw. Not when they were so close to determining whether an eons-old culture was doomed to extermination.

The computer clacked its readiness and belched out the new data. Vrausot snatched up the perforated strip and his massive head swung up and down in satisfaction.

"The orbit's absolutely synchronous," he disclosed. "We can keep the alien landing site under constant observation. And our position is additionally camouflaged by those peaks."

He used the scales of an abbreviated forearm to scratch his lower jaw. With all the authority vested within him as Chancellor of the Shoal, Adviser to the Curule Assembly and leader of the current expeditionary force, he directed the pilot to order gunnery practice.

Assemblyman Mittich swallowed incredulously. "But the aliens! Aren't we going to observe them? That's what we came for!"

"Not now." Vrausot waved him off. "Preparations first. Anyway, we *know* they're aggressive."

"We don't. That's what we have to establish..."

The Chancellor shifted his tail from left to right. "We've observed their machines. They fight among themselves, don't they? And isn't it a fundamental fact of design that automatons are fashioned mainly after their creators, even in matters of temperament?"

"Yes," Mittich admitted. "But we *interfered* with those machines. We interrupted basic behavioral patterns. Our automatons, too, would show primitive social tendencies if the same thing happened to them."

Vrausot exposed a jagged array of teeth that conveyed his displeasure. "I'm in no mood for interference, although I might have expected only forensic exercise from the Leader of the Opposition."

"In that capacity, I'm here to offer suggestions." But it was more than that, Mittich reflected. The Assembly had been quite leery of the compromise plan. The Chancellor had wanted an awesome display of force; the Opposition, a try at peaceful contact.

They finally concurred in: observation, evaluation and application of force *only* if required. And it was hoped that, on the expedition, the Chancellor and Assemblyman would restrain each other.

But how could *anyone* restrain Vrausot?

PREPARE for gunnery practice," the Chancellor directed.

"But," Kavula protested, "that will produce observable emissions beyond the concealment of our shield."

Disappointed, Vrausot leaned back upon his tail. "Very well, then—we'll go through the motions. Order a wet run."

Kavula relayed the order and scores of hatches swung open, baring to space the glistening intensifiers of high-powered weapons. The ship reverberated with the hiss-click articulation of military command and response.

Pivoting on his massive tail, Mittich went over to the teleview screen. "I have your permission, of course, to take a look at the alien vessel?"

"Suit yourself," the Chancellor grumbled.

The screen hunted out and steadied upon the alien ship.

"It's clean!" Mittich exclaimed. "They're *not* armed…"

"Nonsense," Vrausot said, coming over to see. "They've got to be. Why else would they come here?"

"The hull is sleek." The Assemblyman pointed with his long snout. "I see no gun-hatch outlines."

The Chancellor produced the Tzarean equivalent of a humorless laugh. "They're aliens, Mittich—with an alien technology. Perhaps we wouldn't even recognize their weapons if we saw them."

"But, as if they were hostile and furtive, would they have exposed themselves helplessly on that plain—like sitting *uraphi?*"

Vrausot's eyes intensified with resolution. "We're going to strike them—*now!* We're not going to wait and take the chance of having them slip from our grasp."

Appalled, the Assemblyman drew back. "But that's just what we're not supposed to do! We might touch off a war that will annihilate either or both of two cultures!"

"If we don't strike now it'll be our culture that will be annihilated. I wouldn't want that, Mittich. Just think of the glory and honor and tradition of conquest that would be lost forever. What we do here is being watched, indeed, by our ancestors who gave their lives in the final battle for total consolidation of the Tzarean Shoal!"

"But—"

"Our opportunity now is to live up to the finest military examples set by all Tzarean heroes who ever aimed an intensifier out of love for home world. Mittich—*This is a time for empire!*"

It was no use, the Assemblyman saw. Vrausot would have his way. He would wear his shining, imaginary medals and order his attack and bring doom to— oh, how many worlds?

And the Curule Assembly could only give his leadership the support it would need after he presented them with the *fait accompli* of this treacherous deed.

"Kavula!" the Chancellor suddenly hissed. "Order the gunners—"

But Mittich nudged him in the back. "It could be a seine."

"I—what?"

"We may be swimming into a seine. Perhaps they're just toying with us—waiting to see if we are foolhardy enough to attack."

The scales above the Chancellor's eyes stood on edge as he pondered the ramifications of the other's suggestion. Finally, "We'll hold off a while, perhaps."

Mittich had put him off for a moment. But no gain against Vrausot, political or otherwise, was ever more than temporary.

The Assemblyman was jarred from speculation as one of his major scales split with aridity. He hurried off to his isotonic saline tank.

CHAPTER FOUR

RESTED, although no nearer a definite plan for resubjugation of the telepuppet team, Stewart cautiously watched the robots from behind an outcropping. To this concealed vantagepoint he had led Carol, Director Randall, and McAllister while the automatons had been occupied with recharging.

"You're going to try some more voice commands on the OC?" Carol's voice came softly through the earphones as she squirmed to find more comfort within the folds of her oversized sheath.

"We're not doing *anything*," Stewart said firmly, "until that thing is well occupied with transmission."

McAllister's boot came in contact with something hard and he bent down to inspect it. "Say, what's this?"

Randall went over to see. "A burnt-out telepuppet, obviously."

Stewart had a look too. "It's an Algae Detector. But, since there's no water around here, it hasn't had a chance to exercise its function. Electronic atrophy must have set in."

"It's riddled with drill holes," McAllister noted. "Looks like one of those other puppets worked it over."

Stewart examined the thing. The pilot was right.

"At least *one* of our robots seems to have overcome its inhibition against analyzing pure metal," Randall observed, prodding it.

"Or maybe something else has been around here," McAllister said. The director looked up sharply.

"Something else? Like what?" Carol laughed at the pilot's unreasonable concern.

McAllister only hunched his bony shoulders.

It was not difficult for Stewart to see that McAllister was afraid. Neither the pilot nor Mortimer was generally known in the Bureau for his courage. That their apprehension had grown to visible proportions out there on this forsaken edge of infinity was merely an expected extension of their characters.

Rather, it was Randall's fear—Randall's and his own—that concerned Stewart. Both seemed incommunicable. Stewart's reticence was involuntary, stemming as it did from his inability to find words for his incomprehensible dread. And he wondered whether the director's fear, too, was that inexpressible.

He picked tip a clod of soil and crumbled it in his gloved hand, as though symbolizing his anxious desire to come to grips with whatever it was that hid behind a veil in his mind.

Randall lowered himself on his haunches. "Don't we have any *emergency* means of bringing that machine under control?"

"Oh, there are a couple of tricks. Manhandling it is one."

Carol hugged her knees and laughed skeptically. *"That* thing?"

"There's a recessed deactivation switch in its lower section. All I have to do is get my hand on it."

"And all *it* has to do," she retorted dubiously, "is get one of its fifty-pound vises on *you.*"

She seized his hand and, through two layers of rubberized material, he sensed the unsteadiness of her grip. "Do be careful, Dave."

He was impressed. It wasn't often she allowed her more serious nature to show through candidly.

She rose suddenly and turned to face a distant mountain range.

Randall tensed. "Yes, Carol—what is it?"

Profuse light from the primary etched lines of concern on her brow. "I'm sensing electronic spill-off from somewhere up in those peaks—perhaps beyond."

Randall's breath rasped in the earphones. But he only said, "Spurious stuff. Reflections caused by a dense magnetic field can throw you off like that, you know."

She nodded—not enthusiastically, however.

Stewart glanced at the director, who looked swiftly away. But their eyes had met for an instant and, in Randall's, Stewart wondered whether he hadn't detected something cunning, elusive. Or was it just the same nameless fear that he, himself, felt.

THERE it goes!" McAllister exclaimed. "The OC's getting ready to transmit!"

Elbows splayed along the ridge, Carol watched the huge machine steadying its parabolic discs on a spot close to the horizon.

"See if you can pick up some of the spill-off," Stewart urged.

She waved for silence. "I'm beginning to get it now."

"Can you pinpoint the frequency?"

"Just a notch about one thirty-six point two MCs."

"On the nose, isn't it?" Randall asked.

"Close enough. How *are* the signals, Carol?"

"They seem shipshape, well modulated, crammed with data. I can even read some bits having to do with oxygen— plenty of it—in that cave over there, I believe." She pointed, then glanced at Stewart. "There's no malfunctioning at all."

He retrieved his transmitter and switched from MCW to CW. "That simplifies our task. When we re-establish control, all we'll have to do is reorient the OC."

Randall walked several feet away, kicked a stone, glanced up at the sky and returned. "What now?"

Stewart retuned his transmitter. "Penultimate emergency procedure. I'm going to come down with both heels on the frequency at which it received code signals from the relay base."

"But can you give it *coded* commands?"

"I'm just going to lock the sending key on a steady impulse. It's a 'stop-everything' order." He hit the level.

Carol winced. "Ouch. I wasn't ready for that."

"What's it doing now?" he demanded.

"Still transmitting. No interruption."

He released the key. "Well that exhausts our bag of tricks. We'll have to do it by hand."

Just then Carol's amused laughter tinkled in the earphones. "Why, that harebrain machine thinks it's God!"

Randall started. "What?"

"I'm having a peek at its PM&R pack spill-off. It's lord and master of the universe! There's only one thing worthy of touching its pedal pad—the puppet barge. That's because the barge, being metal too, is *a totem!*"

The director shook his head and mumbled, "Most unusual." Then, "Carol, can you see anything at all significant in its memory pack? Any evidence of—"

But in the next instant she screamed and lunged back away from a foot-long metallic crab that had drawn up before her.

"The Flora C&A!" Stewart made a grab for the thing, but it skirted his gloved hand and started forward again.

McAllister backed away until he came up against the outcropping beside the girl. Squirming qualmishly, he kicked out and caught the crab broadside, sending it skittering back.

Then he shouted in pain and gripped his instep with both hands. "My foot! It's broken!"

But, a moment later, Stewart was certain the injury was negligible, judging from the adequate support the foot provided in McAllister's sprint for the *Photon.*

*   *   *

BIGBOSS completed his transmission and turned full attention on the *eureka* signals coming frantically from Grazer.

Interested, he inspected the sequenced data and took note of the modulation peaks that exactly duplicated the C5H8 parameter.

Grazer had sensed *hydrocarbon!* More important, one of his spectromteric biodetectors was getting a whiff of DNA molecules!

Even those significant findings, however, accounted for but part of the frenzy with which Grazer was transmitting his Impulses. There was much more behind the *eurekas* than that. But all the lesser worker could convey telemetrically was his general excitement, for there were no parameters dealing with the third element of his discovery.

Perplexed, Bigboss pondered this inadequacy of communication between him and his servitor—until a rationalization circuit came up with the recommendation: Tap in on Grazer's direct video system.

He did.

And Bigboss went momentarily irrational as motor circuits fought one another to express the exultation flooding from his evaluation pack. He leaped three meters high. His upper command section turned up a hundred revolutions per minute in triumphant delirium. He extended and retracted his vises, leveled his blaster and spat out a lance of vicious destruction that slashed a concentric trench in the ground about him.

Then he damped all activity and steadied himself with a sober appreciation of the telemetric signals Grazer had contributed. The servitor was confronting three hated non-Totemic mobiles!

They had emerged from their needle! They had come finally to hurl direct challenge at the Supreme Being!

Circuit currents surging once more toward irrational levels, Bigboss calmed himself with dedication to the vengeful destruction of those insolent creatures.

He transmitted a "stop-what-you're-doing-and-follow-me" order and headed into Grazer's telemetric signals. Every twenty meters or so, a discrimination circuit peaked in its erratic pattern and he hurled out a bolt of raw energy, annihilating a boulder here, leveling a rise there, pulverizing an occasional crag.

In his excitement, however, he had neglected the environs-scanning procedure he had devised to compensate for his damaged video sensor. And he didn't realize that, while he had been stabilized for transmission, Minnie had almost reached him in a stealthy advance. But now he was pulling steadily away from her.

Ignoring their order of social priority, the workers converged on the nearby outcropping. Some bore to the right around the rock formation, while others joined Bigboss in a flanking maneuver to the left. The long-legged Maggie and Peter the Meter evaluated the slanted stone as comprising no barrier and proceeded directly over it.

WHEN he finally swung around and brought the contemptuous mobiles under direct visual observation, Bigboss paused to evaluate the situation. It required no small amount of self-control to restrain his motor circuits. But he *had* to. For he was determined the arrogant mobiles would not again reach the sanctuary of their Totem.

Grazer stood before the three creatures, his servo units idling as his transmitter continued to send frantic *eurekas*. And now his excited impulses were joined by those of other servitors who had formed a half circle around the outcropping—Peter the Meter, boasting of excitation of an infrared radiometer; Breather, reporting traces of both oxygen and carbon dioxide in the immediate atmosphere; Minnie, whose high neutron flux instruments were beginning to identify concentrations of calcium, potassium, and carbon.

Sequencing and storing the data, Bigboss sent out a curt directive that amounted to: Do not analyze! Just stay out of the way!

The ring of clansmen remained poised. Several times one of the nonmetallic captives attempted to force its way through the workers, but was pulled back by another mobile.

Bigboss brought up his blaster and loosed a vicious, blinding charge that swamped half a dozen unretracted photometers and pulverized the top of the outcropping. He adjusted his aim, compensating for the crouching, huddled position the interlopers had assumed, and fed renewed energy to the blaster's condenser.

By the next sine wave peak, however, he regretted his pre-occupation with the mobiles. For, at that moment, Minnie's drill head, sweeping through one of his fields of vision before he could discharge the blaster, crashed into video pickup lens Three.

He sprang back, rationalization pack coming frantically to grips with this further loss of visual integrity. Through luck rather than intent, he brought one of his still functioning lenses to bear on the advancing Minnie.

She let her entire drill head fly in a bludgeoning blow, but he parried it with his vise while he reasoned out the modified swivel motion now required to provide adequate coverage with only two lenses.

But the attack had touched off a number of other clashes among socially ambitious workers. Seismo turned on Minnie's exposed flank and sent a pedal disc crashing through her after-analyzing chamber. Sludge spilled out upon the ground.

Peter the Meter swung his boom-and-ball gamma ray detector against Breather's air pouches while Maggie straddled Sun Watcher and proceeded to stomp on one of his telescopic instruments.

In the midst of all this confusion, Bigboss was only vaguely aware that the three impudent mobiles had slipped out of the ring of servitors and were returning swiftly to their Totem.

Infuriated over the imminent loss of prey, he swiveled around in their direction. Again, however, he neglected his defense.

And before he could trigger a charge at the fleeing things, Minnie's drill head whipped around in a level arc that snapped his blaster off at its socket and sent it hurtling across the plain.

As she drew back for another blow, he lunged over and managed to grip her bit in his vise. With a violent twist, he broke it off at the chuck.

Subdued finally, she withdrew.

*   *   *

YOU SAW it, didn't you!" Mittich demanded.

Vrausot scratched his jaw with a rigid talon. "Interesting—that trouble between the aliens and their automatons. What interpretation do you put on it?"

Pivoting on his tail, the other spun around from the screen to face the Chancellor. "That they don't even carry side arms. They had no defense whatsoever against their machines. If they were here looking for a fight, wouldn't they be armed at all times?"

Vrausot expressed ridicule by tracing a circle with the tip of his tapering snout. "Mittich, you amuse me. Only one sunset ago you were bending my tail to make me believe they may be cunning; that they might have strung out a seine for us."

"Yes?" the Assemblyman prompted, expecting more.

"Now I simply extend your own logic back to you. They prepared that drama down there for our benefit—just in case we were watching. They *want* us to believe they are stupid and helpless."

Assemblyman Mittich laced the other with a calculating stare. He was aware of the heavy irony in Vrausot's hisses and clicks and he knew the Chancellor was only deriding him.

"If I was forced to arrive at an alternate assessment, Assemblyman—" Vrausot paused and Mittich braced himself for more scorn. "It would be that the aliens *are* stupid, inept, blundering, defenseless. Actually, it would seem that they must have gained interstellar status only through accident."

"Oh, no. We know *that* isn't true."

Ignoring the interruption, the Chancellor continued. "And they *were* foolish enough to come here unarmed, apparently."

But Mittich broke in again. "If I had attracted more votes in the Curule Assembly, we would have come unarmed too."

"Ah! But we didn't. And do you know why? Because the Assembly really believes as I do, even though they might not have the courage to vote their convictions. That's why I'm going to exercise my own judgment—because I *know* their subliminal disposition in this matter."

Mittich unhinged his jaw conveying dismay. There was no doubt now what the Chancellor's intentions were. Oh, he would probably swim around cautiously for a while. But his final determination was already cloaked with inevitability.

Eventually—how soon?—he would lash out at the aliens with all the ship's invincible firepower. And nothing else could be done to delay that treachery. For Mittich couldn't conceive of another last-*purai* diversion, such as the suggestion that the aliens may have strung out a seine, to forestall the tragedy Vrausot was determined to perpetrate.

Lumbering over to the ship's control panel, the Chancellor directed his pilot: "Advance five degrees westward along our orbital path then restabilize."

KAVULA'S hands darted here and there and the vessel resounded with the *thuds* of great tails thumping down on the deck to maintain equilibrium as new velocity came in surges.

"This will put us below the aliens' horizon," Kavula noted.

"Of course it will," the Chancellor hissed back at the other's impertinence. "And we'll be in such a position that they won't be able to observe our artillery emissions."

He turned to the intercom. "Gun Crew One, prepare for firing."

"Action?" Mittich asked, fearing the worst.

"Of a sort—preparatory." The Chancellor studied the teleview screen and once more directed the gunners:

"I'm designating a target circle on one of those peaks down there. You may fire at will."

He touched a button and a green halo flared on the screen. He adjusted it to encompass the surface prominence he had in mind. The ship shuddered as the gunner punched his firing stud.

Mittich watched the surface erupt in a brilliant display of angry energy—a thousand kilometers off target.

The Chancellor received the fire control officer's apology, together with a request for permission to try again. The latter he denied.

"They evidently need the practice," Kavula advised.

The Chancellor fumed at his pilot's insolence. "They'll do better at close range," he promised. "Meanwhile, I want this ship stripped for action. I've reached my decision. One close pass is all it should take. We strike after sunup."

Desperately, Mittich hurried over and swung his small arms imploringly. "You can't do this thing!"

"Oh, quit being such a floundering minnow! Nothing's going to happen. They're quite defenseless, I'm convinced."

"If that's the case, then you are under injunction of the Curule Assembly to make peaceful contact!"

"Drown peaceful contact!" the Chancellor swore. "I'm supposed to exercise my judgment out here!"

"But—

"Flotsam! There will be no peace. If that's what the aliens wanted, they wouldn't have come out here in the first place. We are going to blast them. And from here we'll go on…"

"Go on?" Mittich repeated cautiously. "Where?"

Vrausot's eyes glazed over and his disarray of teeth were exposed to the gums as he paced the deck and beat his arms against his side in a fit of frantic expectation.

"We know where their relay base is," he explained. "We'll strike that next. Then, capitalizing on the element of surprise, we'll continue to their World of Origin and destroy it outright. On the way back we'll probably knock out one or two other planets."

He turned on a dumfounded Mittich. "The war—if there is to be one—will be short. We'll have only to return to the Tzarean Shoal and muster a fleet before we wipe out the rest of their civilization. And once again ours will be the glory of conquest—such as we have not experienced in, oh, how many millennia?"

CHAPTER FIVE

STEWART woke up shouting the next morning.

Perhaps the nightmare had been brought on by his previous day's experience with the telepuppets. For, in his dream, there had been the OC, again spitting out deadly fire that missed the targets only by inches before gouging great craters in the plain beyond.

Suddenly the master robot vanished, taking all the lesser automatons with it. In the suspenseful stillness that followed, Stewart could only stare in bewilderment at Carol and Randall.

Then it came—the blazing, naked light, together with the stentorian roaring that filled the sky and shook every rock.

Terrified, he huddled with the other two, his eyes searching desperately for some place to hide. But as he spotted each gaping fissure, each yawning cave entrance that might offer concealment, it too vanished. Until they were left with only a smooth, featureless plain extending to infinity in all directions.

Eventually the mighty ships—hundreds of them, it seemed—landed. And down debarkation ramps poured thousands of hideous Harpy-like forms, their gigantic claws magnified in his fancy until they were even larger than the bodies they supported and, by their sheer weight, made flight impossible.

This vast army assembled before its ships in the center of the plain and started forward.

But there was a blur of motion on the right and left extremities of Stewart's field of vision and he watched great, gauzy curtains draw together from opposite horizons, meeting directly in front of him. Like dazzling auroral streamers, they hung from a rod located so high in the stratosphere that it was lost in the blackness of space. Diaphanous though the drapes were, they appeared to be adequate, as if through some magical power, to hold back the horde of vicious Harpies on the other side.

But even as Stewart shuddered with the thought of what would befall Randall, Carol, and himself should the almost intangible barrier fail, the director charted forward and drew the curtains aside.

Instantly, the monstrous creatures poured through.

But in the next moment Randall was beside his bunk, shaking him awake and regarding him quizzically.

DISMAYED over the continued evidence of a lurking, inexplicable fear, Stewart ate breakfast mostly in silence while he cast about for a reasonable interpretation of the nightmare.

It was almost as though the auroral curtain represented a mental veil that hid a horror-filled recess of his mind. The content of that fissure—was it something he didn't want to face? Something he had *intentionally* hidden? Was it actually that Randall could, if he desired, draw back the curtain? Why Randall?

He brought his cup to his lips and almost gagged on an icy bitterness. Carol chided him for his abstraction, dumped the coffee into a disposal slot and gave him a refill.

Randall slapped his thigh. "Well, we still have a telepuppet problem on our hands."

Mortimer sat up sharply. "You're not going to fool around with those damned things any more, are you?"

"Don't see how we can avoid it. We've got several days' repair work on that subspace drive coil—*outside* the ship. That's the only way we can either get out of here or recover use of our long-range transmitter. But I wouldn't want to turn my back on those puppets while they're out of control."

"You won't catch *me* out there again," McAllister vowed.

Randall went over to the external view screen and spent several minutes scanning the sky, bright now with the dawning light of Aldebaran.

"You won't find the puppets up there," Stewart said, finally intolerant of whatever phobia Randall might be pampering.

The director turned guiltily away from the screen. "Anybody have any ideas on what we can do about those robots?"

Stewart went over to a second screen. "After having slept on the problem, I think I might be able to contribute something."

He focused on the telepuppets, attending to their various exploratory chores out on the plain. "Carol gave me an idea with something she said yesterday. We may be able to solve our telepuppet worries within five minutes' time."

"Bring the OC back under control?" The director arched his thick brows. "How?"

"We might succeed in immobilizing it. That'll deprive the other puppets of their source of power. Within a few hours their batteries will drain and we'll be able to go to work on the OC without any possible interference."

He indicated his hostile-atmosphere sheath slumped in a corner of the compartment. "Won't need that. But I will have to have a deep-space suit—heavily shielded against solar storm exposure. You have one aboard, McAllister?"

The pilot nodded. "Standard equipment. But you'll think it weighs a ton. It's designed for null-G use."

Carol's puzzlement drained away. "The suit's *metal!* Which means, as far as the puppets are concerned, that it's *totemic!*"

"That's what I figure," Stewart said. "Wearing it may give me status as one of the boys."

McALLISTER had been right. Against the relentless tug of gravity, the armored suit felt as though it weighed not much less than a ton. Laboriously, Stewart planted one thick-soled boot ahead of the other and moved at a snail's pace across the difficult terrain.

Through a separation between two boulders he could see the telepuppet team. The machines were hard at work, with the Operations Coordinator majestically surveying its charges.

Stewart's legs strained under the great weight as he struggled over a rise and stepped out upon the plain.

Pausing, he stared at the mike recessed in the inner curvature of his helmet. It was dead and his resulting loss of voice contact made him feel lonely and inadequate. But the suit was not equipped with radio, since its wearer would normally be plugged into the ship's intercom system through an anchor line.

Inching across the plain, he closed in on the puppet team. Thus far he had not been noticed.

Cautiously, he skirted the knoll on which sat the Solar Plasma Detector. Even now its boom-and-ball sensor was swinging around to point toward a rising Aldebaran. He was certain he had passed in the SPD's direct line of local sight. But it only ignored him.

Twenty paces farther he gave a wide berth to the Atmosphere Analyzer. Here, too, he had to go directly in front of the thing's video sensor. But the AA obliged by making no move toward him.

So far, so good. But he had approached only those robots that would ordinarily show no interest in him, since he was neither celestial nor gaseous. A minute later, however, when he was cleared through without incident by an indifferent Mineral Analyzer, he was certain his totemic qualifications would bring him to his objective without picking up a challenge along the way.

He crested a rise, trudged between the Astronomical Data Collector and the Seismometer and, more certain of his immunity, stepped over the crab-like Microorganism Collector and Analyzer.

Then he stood hesitatingly before the master robot.

Ports ablaze with luminous evidence of faultless power generation, the huge automaton ignored him. Shorn of its laser intensifier, it appeared somewhat pathetic. But Stewart was inclined to waste no sympathy. It stood swinging its upper command section, first right, then left, to compensate for loss of two video sensors. But he was more interested in the underslung, recessed compartment whose outline he could now see. He had only to flip open the lid and throw the switch in order to deactivate the OC.

Suddenly the thing reacted to his presence. One of its lenses swept over him, stopped, swung back, overcorrected, then steadied. And he couldn't guess what analytical criteria were being applied in the general assessment.

The robot raised its vise-equipped appendage. A hostile gesture? Defensive move? Or merely one of the symbols of communication it had devised during its independent reign?

There was swift movement in the periphery of Stewart's vision and, instinctively, he dropped to the ground as a great clanking form swept past him.

Rolling over, he saw it was the Mineral Analyzer, boring in for another attack. The six-legged automaton drew up in front of the OC and swung its stout drill head in a sweeping arc.

He ducked under the gleaming neck and watched it crash into the bigger machine's lower section, sending it bouncing rearward on stumpy legs. The master robot lashed back, slashing a gaping slit in the MA's neck.

Into this fury of swinging appendages Stewart decided he would have to hurl himself if he expected to immobilize the telepuppet team. As unpredictable as the robots were, he might never get this close to the master automaton again.

The flow of battle, however, made his decision unnecessary. For the grappling machines were now sweeping over the spot where he lay and a huge pedal pad barely missed him as it thudded down.

For a fleeting instant, the recessed compartment was immediately above his head. Overcoming the ponderous weight of his mailed arm, he reached up and flicked open the lid. At the same time he managed to get a finger on and throw the switch.

One final kick by the OC hurled him from beneath the tons of metal. Meanwhile, the thing's thrashing vise caught the MA broadside and sent it flailing backward. Then the master puppet toppled over like a towering tree being felled by an ancient woodsman's chain saw. The ground trembled violently with the impact.

Stewart rose and wiped dust from his helmet's view plate.

The monstrous robot lay motionless, darkened ports evidencing its lifelessness. Close by, the Mineral Analyzer stumbled around in looping circles, one of its gyros atilt. The other puppets continued their work, unaware that when all stored energy was depleted there would be no opportunity to recharge their batteries.

Exhausted, his face filmed with perspiration and his hip aching beneath the dent the big machine had kicked in his armor, Stewart headed back for the ship. But his release from urgency lightened his steps somewhat. Now there would be little to do but wait until the lesser puppets ran out of power.

AN AUTOMATIC erector leveled Minnie's tilted gyro. Another emergency maintenance circuit cut in and compensated for precession. Finally her sense of balance was restored.

Rationalization circuits reasoned out the precise maneuver necessary to bring her upright and she rose upon her motor appendages, expecting at any moment to be bludgeoned again by Bigboss' vise.

Slowly she turned and sent her restricted field of vision sweeping across the ground. And her video lens came to focus on—

Bigboss!

In a most unusual position! And—*motionless!*

He was stretched out on the ground, extensible vise limp as it lay half covered by the soil into which it had dug. One of his antennae was crumpled beneath him while the other was bent and twisted. Hardly able to accept as valid the visual data she was receiving, she transmitted an unwarranted "please-verify-that-instruction" impulse at low volume.

Her evaluation circuit was thrown almost into a frenzy when there was no response. At maximum gain, she repeated the signal.

Still no response!

Cautiously, she went forward and stood over the Supreme Being. She lowered her bitless drill head and nudged one of his motor appendages. Drawing away, she watched it swing back and forth in smaller and smaller arcs until it finally came to rest.

Then she went into a limited ecstasy of reaction. She whirled around in circles until she became afraid she would tilt another gyro. She reared up on her two posterior appendages and thumped back upon the ground. She swung her drill head up and down, back and forth, around. Through her rear slot she exhausted all the sludge from her analyzing chambers.

She had won! She had supplanted Bigboss!

She had climbed to the top rung of the ladder!

And now She was Supreme Being!

That she had been able to succeed, despite Bigboss' overwhelming superiority, was a datum so questionable that she almost decided to reject it before storing it away.

Minnie went into another triumphant dance, but suddenly came to a rigid halt. Her head held high and Her lens aimed in the direction of the non-Totemic mobile that was withdrawing toward its needle.

There was something *wrong* in Her Universe! It was not at all as it had been before She had conquered the Supreme Being!

Tensely, She recalled for review impressions only recently implanted on Her drums. And she recognized immediately what was missing.

The telemetric chatter of all the workers was gone! Nor could she detect the constant exchange of directive and acknowledgment that had always flowed ceaselessly between Bigboss and each of the workers. Yet, all the analyzers were there, continuing their chores as though nothing had happened.

Apprehensive now, she assigned her meager rationalization capacity to the task of deducing the reasons behind the startling change. And many sine wave peaks passed before the judgment was handed back up to her main circuits for storage on a memory drum:

Bigboss had *justifiably* been the Supreme Being! For He had indeed, been Supreme. The workers had voices, of course. But they were isolated voices that could be heard by other members of the clan only because they were passed along by Bigboss.

Minnie's drill head sagged until it rested on the ground.

She was Supreme Being now. But it was only a hollow distinction. For she had fallen heir to none of Bigboss' authority. That authority had been lost forever in the neutralization of charges that had rendered the former Omnipotent One impotent.

What *had* she done? How could she have been so irrational? Why hadn't she more thoroughly evaluated the consequences of her forced ascendancy?

More for consolation than for any other reason, she transmitted a desperate "where-are-you?" impulse to Screw Worm.

The directional signals that returned brought with them a great sense of balance to the circuits in her PM&R pack. She was not, after all, alone! She still held the supplemental function of supervision over her sole helper!

She watched Worm approach, kicking up clouds of dust with the jets that propelled him across the ground on his rolling threads. When he arrived, she sent him a "hold-everything" signal. As he remained motionless before her, she lowered her drill head until she could sense the slight change in capacitance values that indicated physical contact with him.

No, even though she had destroyed the Supreme Being and, by that action, had forever shut herself off from the other members of the clan, she was not alone. She still had her Worm!

But within the limits of those circumstances, she resolved suddenly, she would try to *act* like a Supreme Being!

She drew herself upright and remained rigid while she drove her rationalization circuits at a furious pace.

How *did* an Omnipotent One act?

Judging from Bigboss' behavior, a Lord or Mistress of All Creation should go about destroying non-Totemic pretenders.

Was that what *She* should do?

Realizing the decision would require much more concentration, she retired from the site of operations to consider all the factors.

* * *

HALFWAY back to the *Photon*, Stewart paused and leaned against a boulder, exhausted. The muscles in his legs were flaccid from lifting the great weight of hermetically sealed plating with each step. Now he fully understood that the suit was *not* made for walking.

Ahead, the ship was a beckoning silvery pencil that glittered in the harsh, golden light of Aldebaran and cast its blocks-long shadow on strange, bare soil and rocks.

Then he saw it—the elongated, symmetrical shape that seemed to spring up from beyond the horizon and expand explosively as he watched in dismay.

It was a *ship*—the likes of which he had never seen before! Or, then again—

Bewildered, afraid, he could only stand there trying desperately to pierce the veil in his mind, to equate this incredible thing that was happening now to the inexpressible fear he had felt for weeks.

Meanwhile, the strange ship, gliding smoothly in its horizontal attitude that gave evidence of some highly developed type of antigravity drive, surged forward. Its smooth, dark undersurface, he could see, was broken by twin rows of open ports that extended from bow to stern on either side. And deep within those circular recesses bristled scores of elongated metal structures that could only be—*linear intensifiers for laser weapons!*

Then Stewart realized this could only be another nightmare and he sickened at the horrible prospect of being drawn further into the dream. The ship would land, of course, and out of its hatches would pour streams of vengeful, grotesque Harpies.

But, instead, the sky was lashed by scores of fierce, dazzling beams that streaked from the vessel as it passed overhead.

And he sensed that this was no nightmare, no mere symbolic expression of the vague dread that had harassed his thoughts all along. This was *real!* This was actually happening!

Bolt after bolt rammed down from the open ports, scorching the ground, blasting great holes in solid rock formations, leveling hills, raking huge furrows where before there had been only level soil.

One of the laser beams—perhaps the fiftieth or sixtieth—took the nose section off the *Photon*, leaving only jagged metal as an undignified crown marring its architectural integrity. Another found its mark too, annihilating one of the helpless ship's hydraulic fins and tearing a gaping hole in its engine section. The *Photon* tilted precariously, but somehow managed to remain upright.

Then the assaulting vessel was gone, swallowed from the sky by the ridge of hills over which it had passed in completing its low-altitude sweep.

Minute followed minute in the breathless silence that punctuated the impossible attack. Stewart knew he should be pushing on to the *Photon* to see if Carol and the others had happened to be in the demolished nose section.

But he only stood there, paralyzed. For, as he looked back on the unbelievable action, he realized that the vicious attack had, after all, *come as no suprise to him!*

He had expected it all along...

That must have been the nameless fear lurking behind a curtain in his mind. And abruptly he knew with a certainty that expectation of this assault had been the basis of his indescribable apprehension.

He had *known* that a ship—an *alien vessel*—would be here waiting for them!

And the *Photon's* crew would be taken all the more off guard because it was incredible, in the first place, that the galaxy might have spawned two intelligent, star-seeking races within the same sector.

But, if he had had that knowledge, how could he have *forgotten* anything so crucially important?

CHAPTER SIX

STABILIZING itself once more in synchronous orbit, the immense Tzarean ship generated internal gravity and meted out isotonic saline solution to a number of tanks in crew's quarters.

In the central compartment it was a triumphant, impassioned Chancellor Vrausot who turned his massive hulk on Mittich and hissed-clicked, "There! I told you they had come unarmed! There was absolutely no response to the attack!"

Grim-faced, the Assemblyman only stared at him.

Vrausot paced, thumping his stout tail against the deck with each stride. It was a gesture that expressed anxiety.

"Don't you see what that means, Mittich? They *knew* we would be out here. They had independently corroborating evidence to that effect. Yet they came unarmed. They *are* a peaceful, naive, unsuspecting race of sitting *uraphi!*"

Very weakly, the Assemblyman reminded, "Our purpose, then, is to make amiable contact and determine—"

It was no use, though. The Chancellor wasn't listening. He had absolutely no sense of honor or ethical appreciation. But, Mittich reflected, that should have come as no surprise. It was to have been extrapolated from the Chancellor's political history. And now the distressing fact had to be faced: Vrausot was a megalomaniac.

The Chancellor drew proudly erect and his tail stiffened. "But *we're* not weak! Kavula—see that all gun crews stand by. We're going to finish them off now that we've established their inability to inflict damage on us."

Mittich drew back, appalled at the fierce determination behind the Chancellor's driving ambition for conquest, disgusted with his own inability to turn Vrausot's purpose aside. How to stop him?

It was Mittich who paced this time, helplessly wrestling with the impossible problem of preventing the Chancellor from compounding Tzarean dishonor.

Frustrated, he pivoted on his tail and returned to the teleview screen. Focusing on the landing site below, he zoomed in for an extreme close-up. The aliens were still scurrying around outside their crippled ship, glancing occasionally into the sky as though terrified over the possibility of another assault.

Mittich adjusted the instrument to its operational limits, as he had wanted to do on so many occasions since they had brought the aliens under observation.

Two of the creatures were facing the mountain range behind which hid the Tzarean ship. Anxiously, the Assemblyman moved in and studied their heads, clearly visible through transparent helmets.

He drew in a startled breath. He must be mistaken. Of course he was. He could see that now.

Yet, there *was* something fascinating as he compared one of the heads with the other. What impressed him most was the contrast. There was an indisputable difference—many differences. Then he tensed with sudden realization. Perhaps he *could* forestall their fate.

CHANCELLOR," he called out softly. "Don't you think it might be a good idea to take prisoners?"

"Drown the prisoners!" Vrausot swore. "We don't need them."

"Yes, I realize that. But—well, look at the screen."

The other studied the picture. The scales of his forehead strained erect as he pondered the contrast Mittich had already noticed.

"Observe the one on the left," the Assemblyman suggested.

Interested, Vrausot then bent forward. "You don't suppose—?"

"Yes, I do. This is our chance to study *both* sexes."

"I—" The other hesitated. "There could be significant psychological differences, you realize." Mittich pushed ahead while he had the other's attention. "Why, we can't even be sure which is dominant."

The two alien creatures had gone out of the picture, leaving only an empty image of soil and rocks.

"It would be nice to display a *pair* of them at the Curule Assembly, wouldn't it?" the Chancellor said thoughtfully.

"That's what I had in mind. A positive demonstration of our superiority. So much more convincing than empty hisses and clicks."

Vrausot drew himself to his full height. "It will be done. Kavula, assign twenty men to a landing party to accompany myself and Mittich out on the surface. A stun gun for each man."

The pilot turned from his controls. "You'll need something heavier than that if you're going among those machines," he said officiously.

Vrausot displayed his teeth in an expression of uncertainty.

"But the robots won't be a factor for very long," Mittich pointed out. "The principal one has been deactivated. The others depend upon it for their power. Soon they'll be immobile too."

"How soon?"

"By next sunup, I'm sure."

"Very well. We'll go asurface then." Vrausot withdrew for his isotonic soaking.

Mittich turned back to the view screen and worked with its controls. Finally he located the aliens—five of them—trudging across the ground. They were headed for a nearby cliff in whose face yawned the mouth of a cave. It was the same cave one of the automatons had reported filled with oxygen. And he further recalled that oxygen was the basic requirement of the aliens, just as it was the Tzareans' fundamental necessity too.

Evidently they feared another assault on their ship. For they were carrying a number of supplies.

"You don't much approve of what the Chancellor is doing?" Kavula asked, drawing Mittich from his troubled thoughts.

"*You* do?"

The pilot flicked his tail rashly—a gesture usually associated with independent thought. "If he pushes on into the alien sector, it will be genocide. Those creatures are helpless. It isn't the sort of operation I'd care to be in on. Anyway, there's no reason why Tzareans and the aliens can't live side by side, even in one small pocket of the galaxy. We have different requirements. I don't think they would even be interested in the type of world we need."

Mittich eyed the pilot gravely. "We *could* assume command from the Chancellor."

"You do that. I'll watch. There are just enough glory hunters in the Assembly to have my head if I tried and failed."

And Mittich was intensely dissatisfied with himself over the fact that he, too, valued his head dearly.

* * *

ALDEBARAN FOUR, rising in all its primrose splendor, cast eerie splotches of light among the tumbled rock formations outside and thrust a brilliant planet beam boldly into the small cave.

McAllister and Mortimer were huddled against the wall, still assuring each other it must have been some mistake, that there just *couldn't* be an alien race anywhere around.

Randall sat glumly on the emergency transceiver set, salvaged from the *Photon* in order that they might contact a rescue ship—should they be able to hold out long enough for one to be sent.

Still in his suit of armor but minus the helmet, Stewart sat trance-like near the cave entrance. He hadn't said a word in hours. Nor had he uttered half a dozen words since the attack.

Beside him, Carol murmured, "It's going to be all right, Dave. Everything's going to be all right."

She placed a hand on his forehead, then looked worriedly at the director. Stewart, however, wasn't even interested in the fact that she had misinterpreted his numb silence.

For the thousandth time he searched his mind for all its hidden knowledge on the alien space ship, on how he had gained that information, how he could have forgotten it.

Carol tried to console him again, as though he were a child. "We'll get home all right. Then we'll get out of the Bureau. We'll go to Terra—you and I—and you'll see how happy we'll be."

On any other occasion, those words would have sent him into handsprings. But now they just bounced off his traumatic shield.

Then, suddenly, he had it. He *knew* what had happened. He rose, fully in command of himself finally, and struggled out of the heavily-shielded space suit. Then he faced the others.

"I've known all along," he said, "that we might be attacked out here by an alien ship."

Carol gasped. McAllister lunged erect. Mortimer, puzzled, started forward. But Randall stopped him.

"Wait," the director urged. "We may want to hear this."

"I said," Stewart continued, "that I knew it all along. But I didn't *know* I knew it."

He looked away from their bewildered expressions. "Harlston and I made an advance exploration trip to the Hyades, all right. However, we *didn't* find seven—or was it eight?—Earth-type worlds. We didn't even drop back into the continuum. Because we found evidence of bustling sub-space travel and communications that indicated a vigorous culture of star-traveling Hyadeans!"

McAllister swore. Mortimer came forward, perplexed. "But—"

Randall motioned for silence. "Let him finish."

"We got the hell out of there," Stewart said, "without even having seen a Hyadean. We figured that if there was another intelligent race in this part of the galaxy, it might be a hostile one. And our worlds had to know about it. We couldn't chance being captured.

"So we started making subspace leaps back home. One of those jumps ended here—where we had dropped off the telepuppet barge on our way out. At long range, we had a look at that team. And there was an alien ship down there— maybe the same one that attacked us this morning. It could only mean that the Hyadeans were expanding into our sector of the galaxy."

Stewart paused and stared at the cave floor, still confused over what had made him forget all that. Then he went on, but only surmising the rest:

"Don't you see? That ship must have captured us— removed from our minds the fact that we had discovered their nest in the Hyades. That way, we would never suspect we were about to run into opposition in our expansion. We'd be caught off guard, while the Hyadeans would have time for arming…"

Again, he paused uncertainly. "They must have also planted the false impression that there were many Earth-type worlds in the Hyades—so they could pick us off, ship by ship, as—"

But Randall was shaking his head miserably.

NO, DAVE," the director said finally. "The Hyadeans did not brainwash you. *I* did. I also planted the false impression—to justify this mission. It was necessary that only *I* know the true situation."

Stewart staggered back.

"Yes," the other went on, "after you and Harlston told me there was another culture out there of undetermined size and intentions, I almost hit the panic stud. Two cultures expanding toward each other, previously unaware of each other's existence. The wrong move could be the shot heard around the galaxy.

"What to do? Report it to higher authorities? No. For I saw immediately what would happen: 'menace from space'; Terra and Centauri Three, our other worlds—'helpless before an unknown terror'; all that sort of stuff. Anybody could appreciate what the consequences would be.

"Send out a single ship to try for peaceful contact? But who would buy a scheme like that? Instead it would have been: Send out a thousand ships armed with laser intensifiers of every caliber, all manned by green, trigger-happy kids who had never fired a shot in battle back to the eighth generation before them."

Stewart realized there was no reason not to believe him. For all along Randall had acted as though he *expected* to run into something like an alien ship.

The director lowered himself wearily onto the transceiver and folded his hands. "Anyway, from what you reported, I had hopes that there *could* perhaps be peaceful contact—between two single, unarmed ships. The evidence seemed to point in that direction.

"There were our telepuppets, for instance. The OC had quit transmitting—a year ago. Later you tell me you sighted an alien ship on Aldebaran Four-B. If you put two and two together, you come out with something that looks like a logical four."

He fished for his pipe, stuck it between his teeth, but forgot to light it. "If we have hostile aliens working in our direction and planning on surprising us, would they interfere with our robots? Of course not. For then we would send a trouble-shooting gang out here to put the puppets back on their strings. And we might discover them and mess up their strategy.

"So, since the Hyadeans weren't aware you had discovered them in their own cluster, the malfunctioning telepuppets could mean only one thing: They had stumbled upon our robots, reconciled themselves to the existence of another intelligent culture, and *purposely* interfered with the operation of our team."

"But why would they do that?" Carol asked, perplexed.

"As I figured it, that action practically amounted to an engraved calling card—requesting our appearance in the interest of amiable relations."

His final words rasped in his throat and he added remorsefully, "But I was wrong—oh, so wrong! It was only a trap. They just wanted to get us here so they could fire their opening shots!"

MCALLISTER cut loose with a string of expletives. Mortimer only shook his head despondently.

Carol spread her hands. "But why didn't you tell the rest of us what we were getting into?"

Randall laughed in self-disparagement. "Oh, it was part of my grand strategy. I didn't want anybody along who knew what the real setup was. If this was going to be a try for peaceful contact, there'd be no room for possible hostile predispositions built up during nerve-wracking weeks of suspense while traveling to Four-B.

"You see, I even allowed for the possibility that the aliens might be telepathic, or at least have long-range instruments which could dig into our minds. If so, I was determined they would find nothing there to touch off an incident. I went out of my way to pick McAllister and Mortimer, who wouldn't *fight* their way out of a torn paper bag. I didn't want any trigger-happy, eager Bureau boys who might start fissioning at half critical mass."

The pilot and ship systems officer grumbled, but sat still.

"I wanted you along, Dave," Randall went on, "because you are dependable and reasonably pacifistic. And since you already knew, subconsciously, what the setup was, you'd be useful. Because if trouble developed it would break your conditioning."

"And Carol." He smiled at the girl. "I brought her because I was aware of the tender sentiments between you two—perhaps even more aware than you yourselves were. If those Hyadeans *could* see inside us, they'd know something of our gentler sentiments."

Randall snorted. "But I guessed wrong. My entire strategy wasn't worth the brain it was dreamed up in. I led us into a trap. It was the Hyadeans who turned up in a ship bristling with laser weapons. They had not, after all, sent us an engraved come-and-get-acquainted card. Instead, it was come-into-my-parlor."

Stewart was still having difficulty getting it straight in his mind. Somehow, it seemed there were still unanswered questions. But he felt too numb even to wonder about his dissatisfaction.

"The upshot of everything," he said, "seems to be that we've had it. Even if that Hyadean ship doesn't finish us off, there's no way we can get a warning back home."

The director smiled finally. "Give me credit for at least one redeeming bit of foresight. I *did* conceive of the possibility that something like this might happen. So when I conditioned you and Harlston, I arranged it that the conditioning would break down in another three weeks. Harlston will then report everything. And the Bureau will guess why they haven't heard from us."

*   *   *

TO MINNIE'S utter confusion, the great pink sphere had risen yet there had been no subsequent Pilgrimage to Totem. She spent an eternity, it seemed, pondering that enigma but getting nowhere.

Eventually Screw Worm erupted from the ground—oh, so slowly, so sluggishly—and rolled toward her with his load of mineral specimens. When he tried to force the substance into her intake slot, however, she only turned away dispiritedly, still mourning the loss of communication with all the others.

Screw dropped his specimens and squirmed around, tilting feebly into the attitude for boring down again.

His jets came on weakly, managing to rotate him only three or four times before giving out completely. Then he fell into a strange motionlessness.

Minnie prodded him with her chuck. He toppled over, but did not stir. Disturbed, she sent a "report-your-location" command.

But there was no response.

Like Bigboss, he was totally inoperative. Like Peter the Meter and Maggie and Grazer and Breather and all the others, he, too, was now a victim of the stubborn stillness.

Confused, Minnie stumbled forward, realizing that her motor circuits were not responding as lively as they always had. She, too, was having some difficulty evaluating and rationalizing.

Then an odd thought occurred to her: She had devoted most of her time since becoming Supreme Being to considering how she should act. Her motor activity had been at a minimum. The other members of the clan, on the other hand, had continued their physical tasks. And now they were all motionless. Only she had any power left. Could the formula be: Motion minus the presence of Bigboss equals eventual immobility?

If that were the case, then how hollow, indeed, was the distinction of being the successor to the Omnipotent One!

If she was going to act like a Supreme Being, she decided suddenly, she would have to do so in a hurry. But do—*what?*

Then she finally hit upon the answer: She must be about Bigboss' work of destroying non-Totemic pretenders.

And she knew just where to find *five* of the despicable things!

CHAPTER SEVEN

EXHAUSTION blunting the bite of sharp rocks into his back, sleep finally overtook Stewart. Despite his plight, he had not resisted. For weeks had passed since his slumber had not ended in terror brought on by some form of the horrible nightmare.

But it would be different now. The Hyadean ship had torn aside the curtain behind which the suppressed knowledge had lurked. And his subconscious was rid of its awful burden.

He had been wrong, however. He knew that much when the army of hideous monsters sprang up from subliminal depth to fill the cave with their vile, menacing forms.

Only, it wasn't a cave in which he found himself now. It was a huge chamber whose vaulted ceiling was supported by ornate columns. In the center of the room was an immense table, surrounded by thousands of—chairs? Standing on stout legs evidently intended to bear ponderous hulks, the artifacts consisted of paired buttock rests merging into a large, tapering chute that curved down to the floor.

It was as though the chairs had suggested a shape for the monsters in his nightmare. For abruptly the chamber was filled with scaly creatures only remotely resembling the Harpies of his former fantasies. The head was a grotesque pair of jaws, lined with jagged teeth and resembling that of a massive crocodile. Resting in each chute was an immense tail that seemed as large as the body itself.

Then he was caught up in a vortex of blazing light and incredible sounds. He spun from fear to terror, from incomprehensible concepts to semantic confusion. The air about him was a sonic battleground of *hisses* and *clicks*. But, occasionally, one of the noises seemed to convey meaning of a sort.

THE CAVE floor jolted beneath him and Stewart instantly sprang up, welcoming the abrupt awakening no matter what new complication had caused the tremor-like shock.

Then Carol screamed and lurched back against the far wall.

There was a blur at the mouth of the cave and the Mineral Analyzer's huge drill rammed in—until its forward test chamber was blocked by the narrowness of the entrance.

Backing off, the robot charged again; withdrew and came forward once more. Then, apparently satisfied it couldn't get through, the thing directed its drill head in a series of determined, chopping blows that sent fragments of rock hurtling in all directions.

McAllister sidled along the wall. "That thing's got the same compulsion the OC had! It's trying to reach us!"

Randall stood in front of the transceiver to protect it from flying chips. "But I don't think it'll get through," he said uncertainly. "How does it look to you, Dave?"

"All depends on the amount of power it has left." Stewart drew Carol farther from the entrance.

Between blows, he glanced outside. Dawn was beginning to tinge the sky. "But it's been almost a whole day since it's had a recharge from the OC," he added hopefully.

The MA's drill head slammed down again and knocked loose a section of rock the size of Mortimer's head.

Carol dropped to the floor and sat with her arms wrapped around her knees.

Stewart leaned against the wall above her. "You said something about leaving the Bureau—maybe going to Terra—you and I—"

Her face was rigid, though no less attractive than he had remembered it when good-natured jest was her principal mannerism. "Talking about that is only an exercise in futility now," she said.

"I won't argue that point. But I want you to know the words weren't wasted." He took her hand. "It was something I've had in mind a long time."

Abruptly he realized the MA was no longer chipping away at the cave entrance. When he looked up, the robot was withdrawing toward a mound of tumbled boulders perhaps a hundred yards off.

He slumped down beside Carol, his sense of relief dulled by renewed concern over the nightmares. Had *everything* in his subconscious come to the surface? Could there be more?

Carol gripped his arm and he looked off in the direction of her extended finger. Seeping in through the entrance, the gathering light of day was dimmed by a dark form descending silently to the surface.

He lunged up. "The Tzarean ship!"

But it wasn't until several seconds later that he realized he had used two *clicks* of his teeth and a *hiss* to pronounce the strange word between "the" and "ship."

CHANCELLOR VRAUSOT was even more imposing in his home-environment suit. The helmet made his head seem twice as large and the clear-plastic snout cup enormously magnified his craggy teeth.

Just inside the main hatch, Assemblyman Mittich regarded the other and swallowed a strong taste of neglected opportunity. He had soaked awake all night, trying desperately to muster the will to accuse Vrausot of malfeasance and assume command.

But he had to face the bitter fact that he lacked sufficient courage. And, even more distressing, his cowardice was something he would have to live with for the rest of his life— as he watched the destruction of many worlds and billions of their inhabitants.

Odd, he thought, how so much could hinge on a single twist of circumstance. Vrausot would return to the Shoal and become a symbol around which Tzarean determination would rally.

On the other hand, if he, Mittich, were leader of this expedition, he too would receive a hero's welcome. Only, his praises would be hissed in the same breath with glorious tribute to the concepts of peaceful contact.

Vrausot turned to check the readiness of his landing party.

"All stun weapons loaded and set?" he asked, his voice sounding coarse both in Mittich's earphones and through a bulkhead speaker.

He received twenty affirmative tail flicks.

Of the pilot, standing by the hatch control switch, he demanded: "Status of the aliens' robots?"

"They are *all* impotent," Kavula reported back into the bulkhead speaker. "The last one used up its remaining power as we descended."

Vrausot stepped toward the hatch, but hesitated again. "Kavula, you will double check the detention compartment and see that the proper protein nutrient is being synthesized."

The pilot acknowledged with a thump of his tail and opened the hatch.

A short while later the landing party was making its way across the plain toward the area strewn densely with boulders and the cave in the cliff beyond. Formality was strictly observed. Vrausot went first. Twenty paces behind him came Mittich; then, at intervals of ten paces, the remainder of the detail.

*　*　*

FOR MINNIE, impotence was a strange and bewildering sensation as she stood paralyzed out among the boulders.

Equilibrium gyros spinning too slowly to accomplish their function, she had tilted over against a rock. In a final and desperate spasm, her drill head had swung upward, toppled over, fallen a few centimeters and come to rest precariously against a ridge.

Frantically, she fought relentless inertia. She opened special circuits that would ordinarily have flooded her balancing system with emergency current. But servomechanisms failed to respond and her chrome-plated neck remained thrust toward a sun now well up in the sky.

Gears whirred faintly and her head turned ever so slowly on its axis, bringing its video sensor to bear on the cave entrance.

It had been her determined efforts to reach the non-Totemic mobiles, she reasoned, that had drained off all her energy. She had been aware of the imminent power failure even during her last, frantic blows at the rocks. Then, retreating, she had struggled desperately against terrifying paralysis.

And now she stood almost powerless, whereas before her forced ascendancy she had imagined she would be *All Powerful*. It was an ironic turn of fate indeed. Oh, how she longed now for the telemetric voices of the clan, the crisp orders from Bigboss, the obedient, sometimes plaintive responses of Screw Worm to her own directions.

Incapable of movement, she sensed finally and with much distress that her rationalization processes themselves—were becoming—sluggish, weak. She could hardly—think coherently—or with rapidity—any longer.

Slowly her head responded to the pull of gravity and turned once more on its axis, the weighty chuck arcing down like a pendulum. It reached the nadir of its swing and momentum carried it up in the other direction. In a desperate effort, she locked the servo unit.

In that position, her video lens took in the huge, new symmetrical form that had come to rest out on the plain.

It was—another Totem! And approaching—in her direction now were—many other non-Totemic creatures— somewhat different in form—perhaps, from—the ones Bigboss had—pursued. But—still insolent, despicable— things, nevertheless.

Was it—possible that she—could still—discharge her— function as—Supreme Being? If they—passed—close enough, it—would require—only one—final—desperate— impulse—to—

*　*　*

WITH the others, Stewart crowded into the cave entrance, careful not to let Carol press too far outside where she would no longer be in the stream of oxygen flowing from the bowels of the satellite.

"They're coming!" McAllister exclaimed, withdrawing. Mortimer retreated with him, striking out for a small passageway that fed from one of the side walls.

Stewart strained forward, shading his eyes against the glare of Aldebaran. The landing party's advance was half-concealed by the mass of rocks and outcropping's that hid most of their ship. Only occasionally could he see part of a spacesuited Hyadean form as its clumsy, swaying stride brought it more completely into his line of sight.

And vision was further complicated by the glint of sunlight off the Mineral Analyzer's upthrust drill head, which had finally come to rest against the rock.

Carol tilted her head attentively and frowned. "I'm picking up the *oddest* radio stuff. The modulation breaks down into nothing more than clicking and hissing sounds. I can't seem to get any meaning. It's too—alien."

Randall reached back into the cave for his hostile-atmosphere sheath. "I'm going out there and see what happens. After all, I'm responsible for our predicament."

But just then the first alien figure pulled into view, coming around the boulder and pausing. Apparently sighting Randall's movement in the cave entrance, the Hyadean raised a stubby arm that held a gleaming metal instrument.

Randall pulled Carol back into the subterranean chamber. But Stewart only stood there frozen in bewilderment.

Then the Mineral Analyzer's ponderous drill head slipped from its perch and came plunging down. It shattered the Hyadean's helmet and almost tore his grotesque head off, sending his weapon flying out across the plain.

The creature lay there writhing for a moment, then was still, its hideous crocodile head turned lifelessly toward Aldebaran.

Stewart, his eyes locked hypnotically on the prostrate form, could only watch with shocked fascination as the other members of the landing party appeared from behind the rocks. They stood silently around the body, then turned back toward their ship.

"Tzareans"—"Tzarean Shoal"—"Curule Assembly"— "Vrausot"—"Mittich"— *"uraphi"*—

Strange words and phrases whirled about in Stewart's thrashing thoughts as a great flood of deeply buried experiences rushed with cyclonic fury into the conscious levels of his mind. And he realized that, just as the sight of the Hyadean ship had swept aside the conditioning Randall had imposed upon him, so was the sight of Hyadeans— Tzareans—hurling aside another, denser curtain of conditioning.

He staggered back into the cave and fell sitting against the wall as all the suppressed knowledge and memories engulfed him.

* * *

Stewart and Harlston were seated beside the table in the Great Hall of the Curule Assembly. They were having some difficulty making themselves comfortable in chairs designed to accommodate Tzarean buttocks and tail, rather than support the human form. They were manacled, but only symbolically—with flimsy crepe paper-like handcuffs.

"Our problem," Mittich, the Hisser of the Assembly was saying, "has been clearly defined. We have captured the expeditionary ship of an alien culture that appears to be expanding in the direction of the Tzarean Shoal. We have taken pain to teach its two crewmembers the

rudiments of our language. And we have found that the official alien response to this situation may or may not be hostile."

"Kill them! Kill them!" one of the Assemblymen clicked out as he sprang up on his tail.

The Great Hall resounded with click-hisses of approval and disapproval—an equal measure of each, it seemed to Stewart.

He watched Mittich smile—at least, it passed for a smile in the Tzarean Shoal—tolerantly at the excited Assemblyman.

"Killing our prisoners," he chided, "will not alter the fact that alien expansion is under way in the direction of our Shoal."

Chancellor Vrausot lumbered down the central aisle, defying the independence of the legislature as he had during all sessions which Stewart and Harlston had attended as Exhibits A and B of the "Alien threat" issue.

Whacking his tail against the floor for attention, he stood before the table and hissed vehemently. "We must arm to the limit of our potential. We must dispose of these prisoners. We must attack their centers of civilization before they attack ours!"

Another Assemblyman rose imploringly. "But how can we do that? We haven't fought a war in countless millennia. Once we were many and mighty, as they are now. But while they have grown, we have shrunk. Why, our entire Shoal consists of only two civilized worlds. All the others have long been in decay."

"Oh, we could take them by surprise and inflict much damage on their worlds," Hisser of the Assembly Mittich agreed with Chancellor Vrausot, "But they would recover. And we would be annihilated."

"Then what," the Chancellor asked scornfully, "would you propose that we do?"

"Our choices are enumerable:

One—we kill these captives and prepare a surprise attack. Two— we condition our captives to return to the center of their civilization and report that they found no worlds worth possessing in this sector."

Vrausot reared erect in protest. "But eventually the conditioning will break! They will remember! And their race will then fashion an attack!"

"If we are to assume that they would attack in the first place," Mittich pointed out. "Our prisoners themselves aren't certain whether their race would or would not.

"Three—we could try instilling fear in them. Condition our captives to go back home and report a powerful, vast Tzarean Shoal culture. But that, I suspect, would only drive the aliens into a frantic arming effort. And, once a formidable striking potential is accumulated, use will be found for it—believe me.

"Fourth—we could let them return and tell the truth—that the Tzareans are a declining culture on its last tail, so to speak."

Again Chancellor Vrausot erupted in a series of violent hisses and clicks. "But that might only encourage them to attack!"

"Precisely. So the only course left is Number Five. That is to condition our prisoners to report indications of an interstellar culture in the Tzarean Shoal—nothing precise, nothing definite. Our prisoners will say they made no visual observations. We thus present the aliens with neither the temptation of our actual weakness, nor the fear of our pretended strength.

"At the same time we interrupt communications between them and the robots they have stationed in the system halfway between their center of civilization and ours. We shall hope they interpret that action as signifying we have discovered their automatons and desire to meet them in peace on that satellite.

"We shall go there prepared for friendly contact. If they come unarmed, we shall know there will be no fighting; that perhaps they will even provide the stimulus and inspiration for regeneration of the Tzarean culture. After all, it's a pretty big galaxy and there's plenty of room for two interstellar races."

"But," Vrausot hissed grimly, "what if they come armed?"

"Then we shall know what fate holds in store for us. We will prepare to the limit of our resources and acquit ourselves honorably."

Stewart watched Vrausot thump his tail on the floor in an expression of displeasure.

"The administration," click-hissed the Chancellor, "will agree to that plan with two modifications: one—that the Tzarean ship we send to contact the aliens will itself be armed so that the lives of our brave men will not be jeopardized; two—that the highest administrative authority be appointed to lead the expedition."

*　　*　　*

DAVE! Oh, Dave! What's wrong?"

He opened his eyes and stared up into Carol's solicitous face, "I'm all right," he said numbly.

Randall was tinkering with the transceiver, while Mortimer and McAllister were moving about excitedly in the cave entrance.

"Come see what the Hyadeans are doing!" the latter cried.

Stewart went over. In front of the cave, obscuring the formation of outcroppings and boulders beyond, was a pile of shining, metal instruments that looked like—

"The linear intensifiers off their laser guns!" Mortimer revealed. "They've been stripping them off the ship for the past half hour. And look!"

He pointed off to the side, indicating another mound of weapons that were quite obviously of the class the landing party had worn as side arms. In between the two piles and lying directly in front of the cave's mouth was the body of the Tzarean who had been slain by the fall of the Mineral Analyzer's drill head.

Even as Stewart watched, other Tzareans brought more weapons to add to the two stacks.

"Dave!" Randall's voice sounded excitedly back in the cave. "Come listen to this. I've tuned in on their frequency!"

Stewart accepted the earphones and listened to the clicks and hisses that translated readily into:

"How many gun batteries left?"

"Two more and they will have all been dismantled."

"And the stun weapons?"

"There isn't a single one left on the ship."

Stewart tensed. The questioning voice—it couldn't be—

Anxiously, he picked up the microphone and ignored the bewilderment on Randall's face as he hissed, "Mittich! Is that you?"

And the Tzarean who had practically been his companion during the Curule Assembly hearing phase of his captivity answered with a series of startled clicks:

"Friend Stewart? It's not *really* Stewart, is it?"

THE END

If you've enjoyed this book, you will not want to miss these terrific titles…

ARMCHAIR SCI-FI, FANTASY, & HORROR DOUBLE NOVELS, $12.95 each

D-41   **FULL CYCLE** by Clifford D. Simak
IT WAS THE DAY OF THE ROBOT by Frank Belknap Long

D-42   **THIS CROWDED EARTH** by Robert Bloch
REIGN OF THE TELEPUPPETS by Daniel Galouye

D-43   **THE CRISPIN AFFAIR** by Jack Sharkey
THE RED HELL OF JUPITER by Paul Ernst

D-44   **WE THE MACHINE** by Gerald Vance
PLANET OF DREAD by Dwight V. Swain

D-45   **THE STAR HUNTER** by Edmond Hamilton
THE ALIEN by Raymond F. Jones

D-46   **WORLD OF IF** by Rog Phillips
SLAVE RAIDERS FROM MERCURY by Don Wilcox

D-47   **THE ULTIMATE PERIL** by Robert Abernathy
PLANET OF SHAME by Bruce Elliot

D-48   **THE FLYING EYES** by J. Hunter Holly
SOME FABULOUS YONDER by Phillip Jose Farmer

D-49   **THE COSMIC BUNGLARS** by Geoff St. Reynard
THE BUTTONED SKY by Geoff St. Reynard

D-50   **TYRANTS OF TIME** by Milton Lesser
PARIAH PLANET by Murray Leinster

ARMCHAIR SCIENCE FICTION CLASSICS, $12.95 each

C-13   **SUNKEN WORLD**
by Stanton A. Coblentz

C-14   **THE LAST VIAL**
by Sam McClatchie, M. D.

C-15   **WE WHO SURVIVED (THE FIFTH ICE AGE)**
by Sterling Noel

ARMCHAIR MASTERS OF SCIENCE FICTION SERIES, $16.95 each

MS-5   **MASTERS OF SCIENCE FICTION, Vol. Five**
Winston K. Marks—Test Colony and other tales

MS-6   **MASTERS OF SCIENCE FICTION, Vol. Six**
Fritz Leiber—Deadly Moon and other tales

Made in United States
North Haven, CT
22 July 2022

21684743R00131